Enjoy all of these American Girl Mysteries®:

THE SILENT STRANGER   A *Kaya* Mystery

LADY MARGARET'S GHOST   A *Felicity* Mystery

SECRETS IN THE HILLS   A *Josefina* Mystery

THE RUNAWAY FRIEND   A *Kirsten* Mystery

SHADOWS ON SOCIETY HILL   An *Addy* Mystery

CLUE IN THE CASTLE TOWER   A *Samantha* Mystery

A BUNDLE OF TROUBLE   A *Rebecca* Mystery

MISSING GRACE   A *Kit* Mystery

CLUES IN THE SHADOWS   A *Molly* Mystery

THE PUZZLE OF THE PAPER DAUGHTER   A *Julie* Mystery

and many more!

— A *Julie* MYSTERY —

THE SILVER
GUITAR

by Kathryn Reiss

Questions or comments? Call 1-800-845-0005, visit our
Web site at **americangirl.com**, or write to Customer Service,
American Girl, 8400 Fairway Place, Middleton, WI 53562-0497.

Printed in China
11 12 13 14 15 16 17 LEO 10 9 8 7 6 5 4 3 2 1

All American Girl marks, American Girl Mysteries®,
Julie®, and Julie Albright™ are trademarks of American Girl, LLC.

PICTURE CREDITS
The following individuals and organizations have generously
given permission to reprint illustrations contained in "Looking Back":
pp. 154–155—Spencer Platt/Getty Images News/Getty Images (detail, guitar
display); George Diack/*The Vancouver Sun* (Joni Mitchell);
pp. 156–157—A 1968 Fender Stratocaster in sunburst finish owned by Jimi
Hendrix from 1969–70 (mixed media) by American School (20th century),
private collection/photo © Christie's Images/The Bridgeman Art Library,
nationality/copyright status: American/copyright unknown (Hendrix's
guitar); Walter Iooss Jr./Getty Images Entertainment/Getty Images
(Jimi Hendrix); KEZ750323-A © Bill Graham Archives, LLC and available at
www.wolfgangsvault.com (playbill); pp. 158–159—George Diack/*The Vancouver
Sun* (Joni Mitchell); courtesy of Greenpeace (button); Jonathan S. Blair/National
Geographic/Getty Images (volunteers cleaning beach);
pp. 160–161— © Daniel Beltrá/Greenpeace (cleaning pelican); Christine
Matthews (Snack Shack); courtesy of Arbor Montessori School (quilts)

Illustrations by Sergio Giovine

Cataloging-in-Publication Data
available from the Library of Congress

For my daughter, Isabel,
whose stumble on the stairs
sparked the idea for this story!

Every cloud has a silver lining.

TABLE OF CONTENTS

1   TREASURES ON NOB HILL 1

2   SOMETHING FOR THE BIRDS 19

3   BUMPS IN THE NIGHT 28

4   TROUBLE WITH A CAPITAL T 37

5   A MUSICAL MYSTERY 48

6   A CLEVER COUNTERFEIT 57

7   AT THE VERNON MANSION 70

8   SUSPECTS AND SHADOWS 83

9   FOOTSTEPS IN AN EMPTY ROOM 94

10   TRAPPED! 108

11   HIDE AND SEEK 119

12   COMING CLEAN 129

13   GOOD VIBRATIONS 143

     LOOKING BACK 154

TREASURES ON NOB HILL

Julie Albright sat on the edge of her chair in the elegant drawing room of a mansion on Nob Hill. "Look!" she whispered to Tracy, her seventeen-year-old sister, in the next seat. "Isn't that the mayor? And over there—that's Stella Ethan, the actress!"

"Don't point!" Tracy warned. "The auctioneer might think you're bidding."

Julie kept her hands folded tightly in her lap so that she wouldn't raise one of them into the air by mistake. She and Tracy and their mother were among the throng of people attending an auction on Nob Hill. The room was crowded with San Francisco's celebrities. Eleanor Vernon, an old school friend of Julie's mom's, had kindly opened up her home for the event, which was

1

being held to raise money for sports programs in San Francisco's public schools.

"When will they auction the beaded dress you've donated, Mom?" asked Julie. Mrs. Albright owned Gladrags, a popular shop full of trendy clothing, gifts, and decorative items—some of them handmade by Julie's mother herself.

"I'm not sure, honey," Julie's mom replied.

Mrs. Vernon, sitting with her husband on Mom's other side, smiled at Julie and handed her a program. "Here, the catalogue lists the auction items in order. Maybe a celebrity will buy your mom's dress. It's fun to have a few celebrities here—and local politicians. But I hope everybody else bids on things, too. We want to sell everything!"

"Thanks," Julie said, taking the catalogue from Mrs. Vernon. She admired her mom's elegant, dark-haired friend. Eleanor Vernon, dressed in a pantsuit of lavender linen, moved easily among the celebrities and socialites but was a gracious hostess to her other friends and neighbors, too.

Mrs. Vernon and her husband, Reginald, had arranged the auction for this first Sunday in March. The spring day was sunny and warm, and a good-sized crowd had come to the beautiful home in San Francisco's fanciest neighborhood to raise money at the benefit auction. Julie and other members of her school's basketball team were attending the auction with fingers crossed for luck. The money raised would go toward saving their school's faltering sports program.

Julie leafed through the pages of photos in the auction catalogue until she found her mom's beaded dress. It was the next item up for auction. Maybe whoever bought it would start a trend, and celebrities would flock to the store to buy the dresses!

"Going once . . . going twice . . . sold to the young lady in the blue sequins!" cried the auctioneer.

"That's Teresa Donnell," breathed Tracy. "She's my favorite singer! I can't believe she's here—and buying *your* design, Mom! She is

3

the Hollywood trendsetter."

The young singer who had just bid success-
fully for the handmade beaded dress clapped
her hands in triumph. Bulbs from dozens of
cameras flashed as she walked up to the auctioneer to claim her purchase. Julie reached over
to hug her mom. "It was nice of you to donate
the dress for the auction," Julie said. She was
proud of her mom.

After the auction concluded, the event
chairwoman rang a little bell to get everyone's
attention. "Thank you all so much for coming
and for supporting sports in our San Francisco
public schools," she said. "I hope you will
return in two weeks for our next auction, also
generously hosted by Eleanor and Reginald
Vernon. That auction will raise money to help
the ongoing effort to rescue seabirds injured by
the recent oil spill in the San Francisco Bay."

The room buzzed with approval mixed with
exclamations of anger and disgust at the tanker
accident that had dumped thousands of gallons of oil into the bay. The oil slick had spread

like black poison, polluting the water and killing fish and birds, as well as destroying their habitats.

"Many charities are already helping," the chairwoman went on, "and the proceeds of our next auction will be donated to rehabilitating birds affected as the oil slick continues to spread."

Julie felt upset every time she thought about the careless tanker pilot who had crashed the huge ship into the jutting rocks near the East Brother Lighthouse. All the oil he'd dumped into their bay was spreading with the tides, washing up on beaches and in marshland for *miles*.

"The high school kids are all washing cars next weekend to raise money for the seabird cleanup," Tracy whispered.

"I want my school to help, too," said Julie. "*I* want to help!"

"Maybe that's something the student council president can bring up at the next meeting," suggested Mom with a twinkle in her eye.

"I will!" said Julie, who had been proud to be voted president, though she often felt the meetings didn't accomplish as much as they should. "That's a *great* idea. It would be super cool if we could do something for the auction." She busily started imagining services she and her classmates could auction: house cleaning, gardening, dog walking . . .

While the auction committee tallied up the money that had been raised, the auction chairwoman urged everyone to enjoy the refreshments that the Vernons had generously provided. Tracy dashed off to try to get autographs from the stars, but Julie and her friend T. J. joined the crowd moving toward the linen-covered refreshments table, which held trays full of cupcakes, cookies, and fruit tarts. The Vernons' housekeeper, Ms. Knight, was stationed behind the table, in charge of serving drinks. But Julie noticed that the young woman wasn't really paying attention to her job. Instead she was craning her neck to look at all the celebrities, her big brown eyes wide and admiring. Julie and T. J.

waited patiently for their cups of fruit punch.

"Oh, sorry!" Ms. Knight smiled distractedly at Julie and T. J. and poured their punch. "Did you see Stella Ethan and Teresa Donnell? And that handsome soap opera star, Kevin Woodrow, is here, too! I hear they're going to be filming the next season right here in San Francisco."

"My sister watches soaps, too," said Julie. "I bet she'd love his autograph."

"I'd rather meet the San Francisco Giants' coach," said T. J. "Mr. Vernon is his real estate agent! He promised he'd introduce me."

"I'd rather be introduced to Dick Weston," said Ms. Knight, pointing into the crowd. "He's a TV producer. It's my dream to be an actress someday." Her voice was wistful. She straightened her skirt and patted her afro as if hoping that a perfect outfit and hairstyle would land her a part in Mr. Weston's next series.

"Julie!" Mom beckoned her over. "Mr. Vernon has offered to give us a tour of his collections. Would you and T. J. like to see them?"

Julie nodded enthusiastically as she finished

her last cookie. She and T. J. followed Mom, Tracy, and the Vernons out of the drawing room into the marble-floored entrance hallway from which rose an imposing curved staircase. Mr. Vernon directed them past the stairs into a paneled library.

"Here's where I display my little treasures," the big man said with a jovial chuckle.

"Here and in six other rooms," said his wife with a sigh. "It's a good thing we have a large house, because my Reggie is an incurable collector."

Julie knew that Reginald Vernon was a very wealthy man who had made a fortune in real estate. Now Mr. Vernon strode across the library, pointing like a tour guide to the items on display, and Mrs. Vernon followed in his wake with the others as he described all the artwork, jewelry, and sculptures around the big room. Julie was startled when a cream-colored cat perched atop a high bookcase leaped down onto Mr. Vernon's shoulder and sat there like a fluffy parrot on a proud pirate.

Julie had to smile. But when she reached up to pet the cat, Mr. Vernon raised a warning finger. "Best not to tangle with Mister Precious! He's trouble with a capital T—and known for being rather dangerous!"

Julie quickly put her hands behind her back as the cat glared down at her with scornful blue eyes and settled into Mr. Vernon's arms. *He probably just gives them a hard time as revenge for giving him such a silly name*, she thought.

"Look at this," Mr. Vernon was saying, indicating a tall black hat under a glass dome. "A top hat worn by Abraham Lincoln. See here?" He lifted the dome and gently tilted the hat on its side. "It still has the original hatmaker's tag—*J. Y. Davis*—sewn inside."

Fascinated, Julie moved closer to inspect the hat. The black silk was so old it looked rusty.

"And here we have my most prized pieces," said Mr. Vernon, "my guitars." He gestured to the end wall where eight colorful electric guitars hung on both sides of a massive fireplace.

"Oh, *wow!*" T. J. exclaimed.

Mr. Vernon grinned at him and pointed up at a gleaming silver guitar. "This is my pride and joy. It was once owned by Danny Kendricks— one of the greatest guitar players of all time. At least in my opinion."

"Mine, too," said T. J. reverently.

"Check out the workmanship on this beauty." Mr. Vernon sounded as proud as if he had crafted the instrument himself. "And look how Kendricks restrung the strings—upside down— so he could play left-handed even though it's a right-handed instrument. See here? These scratches on the pickguard were made during Kendricks's wild riffs!" Mr. Vernon shook his head, reaching up to caress the scratch marks. "What a tragedy," he said. "Such a talented young life cut short. I knew him personally, you know. I arranged the purchase of some ocean-front property he wanted back in 1969, just as he rocketed to fame. Then a couple of years later I helped him find an architect to build his home in Sausalito. He knew I was a collector and very generously gave me one of his own guitars as a gift—this Fender Stratocaster. Top of the line!"

"It *was* awful when Kendricks died in that motorcycle crash," T. J. said to Julie. "He was so cool. I want to learn to play guitar the way he did. I'm even left-handed—just like he was."

Julie remembered that her sister had been especially sad about Danny Kendricks's death last year. Tracy had pinned to her bedroom wall photographs of the dreamy, curly-haired singer with his soulful gaze, but took them down after she heard the news of the crash. "I can't bear to look at them now," she'd told Julie.

Mr. Vernon sighed, running a hand lightly over the silver Stratocaster. "It's going to be hard to part with this one at the next auction."

His wife shot him an amused glance. "Oh, Reggie, you own so many guitars, from so many famous guitarists. At one time or another you've said each is your pride and joy! You know selling a few items from your collections will do a world of good for the benefit, and you won't really miss any of this stuff."

"Well, I do agree that the seabird rescue is

an excellent cause." Mr. Vernon winked at Julie as he motioned the group into the next room to look at his collection of baseball memorabilia. "My wife wishes we lived in a little cottage where there was no space for my collections."

Julie giggled. She moved on to examine a bat that had belonged to baseball legend Babe Ruth. But T. J. lingered, looking longingly at Danny Kendricks's silver guitar.

"Reggie likes to tease me, but I *would* like a simpler house," Mrs. Vernon confessed to Julie's mom. "This place is perfectly *huge* for the two of us. And all these collections—room after room of them! I'm telling you, it's like living in a museum." She laughed wryly as they walked around looking at rare china in glass cases, antique models of soldiers, and a whole cabinet full of old cameras. "So much *stuff*," she sighed. "Sometimes I feel like selling off the whole lot while Reggie is away on business."

"That's why he always takes you with him, Aunt Eleanor," joked a long-haired young man as he approached them. "To keep his stuff safe."

Everyone laughed, but Julie noticed that Mr. Vernon gave his wife a sharp glance. Mrs. Vernon introduced the young man as Jasper, their nephew. Julie eyed him with interest. She had heard a lot about this nephew. Whenever Mrs. Vernon stopped in at Gladrags for a cup of tea with Julie's mother, talk often turned to Jasper, the nephew who was living with his aunt and uncle while he tried to figure out what to do with his life. He had finished high school but didn't want to go to college, so he had come to live with the Vernons until he found work. "But he's not looking very hard," Mrs. Vernon had lamented. "Jasper spends his days lounging about the house listening to music, or else he's gone for days at a time, hanging out at Stinson Beach with his friends. And all the while Reggie indulges him with lavish amounts of spending money!" Mrs. Vernon clearly disapproved. "Sometimes I doubt the lazy fellow is even looking for a job. He's the sort who just wants money to appear in his pockets by magic."

As they all headed back to the drawing room,

where the auction crowd continued to swarm around the refreshment tables, the young housekeeper hurried up to her employers.

"Excuse me," Ms. Knight said breathlessly, "but I'm afraid I've had some bad news. I just received a call from my sister. My mother has been taken to the hospital. I know you're going out of town tomorrow, but . . ."

"Oh, Louisa, I'm so sorry," Mrs. Vernon said, putting a comforting hand on the housekeeper's arm. "Of course you must go to your mother! Someone else will look after things here while we're gone, I'm sure. But can we help you in some way?"

"No, thank you, Mrs. Vernon. But I had better go right away." Ms. Knight untied the apron she'd been wearing. "I may have to be away for several days."

"We understand," said Mr. Vernon. "Please let us know if we can do anything."

"Thank you," the housekeeper replied. "I'll just run and pack a few things."

As Ms. Knight vanished down the back

hallway, the big cat in Mr. Vernon's arms leaped suddenly to the floor and twined himself around T. J.'s legs. T. J. reached down cautiously to stroke him, and the cat purred loudly.

"Why, Mister Precious likes you," Mrs. Vernon said to T. J. with surprise. "And he's very picky about his friends." She looked at him. "I wonder if you'll do us a favor? We'll need someone to feed him while we're out of town, since Ms. Knight needs to be away, and Jasper is allergic to cats—and not terribly reliable."

T. J. looked delighted. "That would be so cool."

"We do have a neighbor we could ask if you can't make it," said Mrs. Vernon.

"Mrs. Buzbee's bound to check in anyway," added Mr. Vernon with a laugh.

"Don't worry," said T. J. "I'll be here!"

"Then please stay after the auction so that we can show you how to prepare his special diet," said Mrs. Vernon. "It's a relief to know we can count on you."

The head of the auction committee rang her little bell again to get everyone's attention.

She announced that the auction had raised more than $10,000 for school sports. The room erupted in cheers and applause. Julie and T. J. whooped and hollered, jumping up and down.

Julie was thrilled. "Wow, auctions are a great way to make money," she declared. "And the next one will raise just as much money for those poor birds."

"Or even more!" predicted T. J.

Back home in their apartment, Julie watched the evening news after dinner. The image of a wildlife rescuer holding a baby pelican coated in thick black oil brought tears to her eyes. The reporter spoke about how the oil tanker had sailed into the San Francisco Bay during a thick fog the week before, hitting large rocks and tearing a hole in the tanker. No lives had been lost, the reporter stated, but Julie shook her head.

"What about all the birds?" she said sadly.

Mom gave her a sympathetic look and

switched off the television. "The next auction will raise money to help them," she said. "But in the meantime, don't you have some homework?"

"Just to sketch my design for the school quilt," Julie said. The art teacher had announced a schoolwide project to make a patchwork quilt that would hang in the entrance hall of Jack London Elementary School. Every student would create a square, painted or stitched with a picture of something that made him or her happy. Then some teachers and parents would stitch all the squares together to make a quilt.

Julie reached for her schoolbag and pulled out her sketch pad. She opened it to her drawing of what made her happy: a black-and-white border collie, the kind of dog she hoped to have one day. But now, pencil in hand, she found herself starting a new sketch. This one was of a pelican, white and clean and healthy, standing at the edge of blue water, under a blazing yellow sun.

That night Julie had a hard time falling asleep. She lay awake trying to think of something her school could do to raise money to help the seabirds. Car washes and newspaper drives were good ideas, but she wanted something they could sell at the auction.

We could auction services, like dog walking and cat feeding and gardening, she thought, but it would be nice to involve the whole school, and some of the younger children would not be able to take on those jobs.

She burrowed under her cozy rainbow quilt, tracing the raised pattern of stitches over and over with one finger. Mrs. Wagner, their art teacher, was teaching the children how to embroider and appliqué little pictures for their quilt squares. Someone had made this rainbow quilt, too, with neat, careful stitches and little raised knots. Or maybe it hadn't been made by just one person. Maybe people had worked together...

Slowly, as Julie drifted off to sleep, an idea began to take shape.

2
SOMETHING FOR THE BIRDS

In the morning, Julie was awakened by a clap of thunder even before her alarm went off. She dressed in her favorite calico print dress, red tights, and low boots, and then tied a bandanna over her hair. Hastily she made her bed before heading to the kitchen for breakfast. While she ate her scrambled eggs, Julie stared out the window at the rain and thought about her idea for the auction. The telephone on the wall jangled, startling her.

Tracy reached past Julie to answer it. "Hello? Oh, hi, Maggie. What—really? Are you serious?" Tracy stretched the phone cord as far as it would go while she made herself a piece of toast and continued talking.

Julie listened with interest to her sister's end

of the conversation: "Oh, that's so cool! We'll have tons of fun. Why can't you come right away? The place is empty, far as I know." Julie and Mom looked at each other, raising their eyebrows in joint puzzlement. "Far out!" exclaimed Tracy. "Your parents have earned my eternal devotion!" She said good-bye and hung up the phone.

"Tell us!" ordered Julie.

"Maggie's family is moving into the apartment upstairs!"

"Lucky ducks," Julie said enviously. "You and Maggie both." She wished her own best friend would move to their building! But Ivy Ling lived on the other side of San Francisco, on the same street where Julie had lived before her parents' divorce. Although Julie still saw Ivy every other weekend when she and Tracy visited their dad, it wasn't the same as living nearby. But when Maggie's family moved in, Tracy would get to see her best friend every day!

"That apartment upstairs has been empty

for a couple of weeks now," Mom said. "I'm looking forward to having neighbors again."

"I think I saw the previous tenants only once or twice the whole time they lived here," said Julie. "They seemed friendly, but they were always working or traveling."

"Why did the Ogilvies leave?" Tracy asked. "They didn't live here long."

"They're both artists of some sort." Mom shrugged. "Mrs. Ogilvie shopped at Gladrags a few times. She told me the apartment didn't suit them."

"Mrs. Ogilvie told *me* the apartment didn't have the right feel," said Tracy. She struck a dramatic pose and spoke in a breathy voice. "*Darling*, it just doesn't have the right *vibes*."

Mom laughed. "You sound just like her! Maybe the light just wasn't right. Artists need good light for painting or photography. Or maybe there were too many stairs. I've seen Mr. Ogilvie using a cane from time to time."

"What are *vibes*?" asked Julie.

"Vibrations," explained Tracy. "Impressions.

Leftover feelings in a place."

"I guess artists are sensitive to things like that," said Julie.

"Well, luckily Maggie's family thinks the vibes in the apartment are great." Tracy grinned. "And they're moving in next month!"

"It will be nice to have them here," said Mom. "Now you girls need to hurry or you'll be late for school."

"Pretty please, may I take the car?" begged Tracy.

Mom considered this request. "I suppose so, if you drop Julie off on the way."

"Yay!" Tracy gave Mom a quick hug and then turned to Julie. "Ready, kiddo?"

Pleased not to have to walk to school on this rainy spring morning, and eager to talk to the art teacher about the idea she'd had last night, Julie grabbed her book bag and rain poncho. "Ready!"

At lunchtime, Julie spotted T. J. sitting with their friends Joy and Carla, and she took her tray over to their table. "So, have you started your job cat-sitting for the Vernons yet?" she asked T. J.

"Sure have," T. J. replied.

"Aren't the Vernons those rich people on Nob Hill?" Joy said. Joy was deaf, but this challenge did not stop her from joining conversations. "Don't they own a huge mansion?"

"That's right," said T. J., turning toward Joy so that she would have no trouble reading his lips. "My dad says they own property all over the Bay Area."

"They own our building, too," Julie chimed in. "My mom thinks it's fun having her old school friend as her landlady. It's funny, though, because even though Mrs. Vernon lives in that Nob Hill mansion, she told Mom she likes our place better than hers."

"Maybe she's lonely in all those big rooms," said Joy. "Maybe it's spooky!"

"Speaking of *spooky*," T. J. said, "when

Mrs. Vernon was showing me how to mix the special cat food, a face suddenly peered right in the window!"

"Yikes!" shrieked Carla. "Who was it?"

"Nobody I knew," T. J. replied, "but then Mrs. Vernon told me it was just Mrs. Buzbee, their neighbor, who always wants to know what's going on in the neighborhood. Mrs. Vernon said that ever since Mrs. Buzbee's husband died she's always coming over to ask for a cup of sugar to bake a cake, or to introduce herself to any guests the Vernons have invited over." He grinned. "And Mr. Vernon said that whenever they do invite her in, she tries to snoop in every room. He said he even found her peering into their coat closet once! But then yesterday, when Mrs. Vernon opened the door, Mrs. Buzbee handed over a pair of silver candlesticks for the next auction."

Silver candlesticks would raise a lot of money for the seabirds. Julie decided she might like Mrs. Buzbee after all.

"So did you get to look at those guitars again

before you left?" Julie asked him.

T. J. shook his head. "Nope. Some people were setting up lights and tripods in the library. Mr. Vernon said they were photographing the stuff that's going to be featured in the next auction catalogue."

"Oh, well, when you go after school today, you'll have the house to yourself," Julie reminded him. "You can drool over the guitars for as long as you like."

T. J. made them laugh by playing air guitar and drooling as they got up and emptied their lunch trays before heading outside for recess.

At the student council meeting after school, Julie told the members about the auction to raise money to help the seabirds injured by the oil spill. "You know we're all making a quilt for the school," she began. "But what if we make the quilt to sell at the auction instead?"

Julie had gone to Mrs. Wagner in the art

room before school, explaining her vision of a colorful patchwork of squares, each depicting some facet of ocean life. "Mrs. Wagner thought it was a great plan," Julie told the council members, "but she said if we're going to have one ready in two weeks for the auction, we have to work like *lightning!* Mrs. Wagner and a couple of other teachers will sew all the squares together using sewing machines, if we can get the squares done quickly. When the squares are all sewn together, we'll have an amazing quilt to auction off for the seabirds—made by every kid in the school. It should raise *tons* of money!"

Everybody started clamoring with ideas for what to put on their squares.

"I'll embroider a seagull!" said Karen.

"I'm going to try painting penguins!" said Joy.

"Oooh, what about *sharks*?" asked Jeffrey.

"I'm going to appliqué a ship," Ricky announced. "A pirate ship!"

"Do the pictures have to be realistic?" asked Karen.

Julie shrugged. "I think the pictures can be

real or imaginary—as long as they're related to the ocean." She looked around at everyone. "So, what do you think? All in favor of this project, raise your hands!"

Enthusiastic hands waved in the air. Everyone wanted to donate the school quilt to the auction.

Julie smiled. "That's great! Then let's get to work."

Then everybody started making a list of all the things they could think of to do with ocean life, and Carla suggested they make copies to give to all the classes. Their voices rose and fell, and Julie listened with quiet optimism.

She felt in her bones that it was going to be a successful project. *Good vibes!* she thought. *Our quilt will be so beautiful, it will raise enough money to rescue every single bird.*

3
BUMPS IN THE NIGHT

Late that night Julie's eyes flew open. Her bedroom was dark. Had a clap of thunder awakened her as it had that morning? She lay listening to the gentle rain against her windowpanes. Then she heard a thump overhead. *That* was what had pulled her from sleep.

Just noise from the apartment above, Julie determined sleepily. She started to roll over and then had a sudden thought: the Ogilvies had moved out of the apartment upstairs, and Maggie's family had not yet arrived. Still another thump sounded in the empty apartment, and Julie glanced at her alarm clock. She had gone to bed at nine o'clock, and now it was just past midnight. What could be making the noise? With a shiver, she remembered what the Ogilvies had said about the apartment's bad vibes.

Julie lay still, straining to hear, telling herself she should get up and ask her mom about the noise. But there were no more thumps. Her eyes felt heavy, and the patter of the rain was soothing. Soon Julie was asleep again.

"Are vibes like ghosts?" Julie asked at breakfast the next morning.

"Not really," said Mom.

"Well, I heard noises last night from upstairs."

"Probably just the cleaners. Getting the place ready for Maggie's family."

"At midnight?"

"Or maybe the Ogilvies came back. Their lease isn't up till the end of the month."

"That's why Maggie's family isn't moving in until *next* month," said Tracy.

"Don't you worry about vibes," added Mom. "It's just the way some people talk—nothing supernatural."

"I'm not worried," Julie said. "I just don't like things that go bump in the night!"

At school, as Mrs. Duncan wheeled a projector on a metal cart down the middle of the aisle, Julie tried to catch T. J.'s eye, but he sat hunched in his seat without looking at her.

Mrs. Duncan pulled down the screen to cover the chalkboard. "For our science lesson today," she told the class, "we're going to watch a film to learn more about oil spills and how they affect the environment." She directed two boys at the back of the room to close the curtains.

Julie watched with interest. The film began with footage of ocean waves rolling onto white sands. Then it cut to sailboats in a bay, their colorful sails flapping in a brisk wind. Seagulls wheeled overhead.

The camera moved lower to take in life on the beach—scuttling crabs, hopping sandpipers—and then zoomed lower still, until it was filming underwater caverns swarming with fish.

"When an oil spill pollutes the ocean," a man's deep voice began, "it becomes unsafe for people to swim, or to play at the beach. It's also dangerous for the creatures that count on the beach and ocean for their habitat. Birds' feathers can become clogged with oil, and the birds cannot swim or fly. If their entire habitat is oil-covered, including the fish and plants that they eat, then many thousands of birds may die unless they are helped."

Julie winced at the picture on the screen—a pelican coated in black sludge. Feebly it tried to raise its wings, but they were too heavily soaked with oil. The pelican's round black eyes stared helplessly at the camera. "Cleaning this one bird takes over 300 gallons of clean water in a gentle soap solution," the narrator's deep voice continued. "Each bird needs dozens of baths to slowly dissolve the oil so that it can be washed off. The birds also need to be given liquids and antibiotics. It's a painstaking job to clean even one bird—and yet there are thousands affected by an oil spill."

The film went on to show how caring volunteers helped veterinarians and scientists clean the birds and remove the spilled oil from the ocean and beach. Julie watched with wide eyes as the pelican was restored to health.

Mrs. Duncan switched off the projector and motioned for a student to turn on the lights. Then she smiled at Julie. "Julie, would you like to tell the class about the student council's plans to support the oil cleanup efforts in the bay, and how each student can contribute?"

Julie was still a bit shaken by the images she had just seen in the film, but she stood up tall and described how the quilt project had become a fund-raiser, to be sold at a benefit auction to support the oil-spill cleanup efforts. Although the film had upset her, Julie felt proud to be doing something to help all those poor birds.

At recess, Julie climbed the jungle gym with Carla. As they pulled themselves up to sit at the very top, Julie could just see the glimmer of the water in the bay, which looked, at this distance, as if there were no oil staining it at all.

"Wasn't that film sad?" Carla asked. She pulled her transistor radio out of her jacket pocket and turned the dial until some music started playing. "Maybe this'll cheer us up."

"Hey, that's Danny Kendricks," Julie said, recognizing the husky voice. "T. J.'s favorite musician." She listened to the beat of the music, but it didn't cheer her up. All she could think of was the image of the frightened pelican smeared with black oil.

"I still can't believe the tanker pilot didn't see those rocks," she murmured.

"It was foggy," Carla reminded her.

"Well, my dad uses radar when he's flying through heavy cloud cover," Julie pointed out. "Why didn't the boat captain use the ship's radar to help him navigate through the heavy fog?"

Carla shrugged. "I guess sometimes people just make mistakes." She turned up the radio. "This is a cool song!"

Sitting atop the jungle gym, Julie and Carla pretended to be a rock band. Julie fluttered her fingers and mimed playing a keyboard while

Carla pounded imaginary drums, but it wasn't the same without T. J. on air guitar. She wondered why he hadn't come to sit with them as he usually did. She could see him all alone, kicking a ball against the chain-link fence.

After school, Julie looked for T. J., but he hurried away before she could ask him what was wrong. She walked home, eager to work on her new quilt square design.

At home, Julie found that Tracy was out with friends and Mom was working downstairs at Gladrags. Julie helped herself to a snack and sat down at the kitchen table to get her homework out of the way. After her busy day at school, Julie enjoyed being alone in the quiet apartment. There were no sounds except for occasional voices and car horns out in the street.

When Julie finished her homework, she went to her room. She took out her sketch pad and flipped through pages of sketches of her dream dog—a black-and-white border collie with floppy ears. Unfortunately, most of the drawings looked more like horses than dogs. Finally she came to the little drawing she'd made of the pelican under the bright yellow sun. Sprawled on her bed, Julie started sketching little sunglasses on the pelican.

She could hear her bedside clock ticking. She reached over to turn on her radio, but before her finger pressed the On button, Julie heard another sound—a series of thumps. And then footsteps in the empty apartment overhead.

Ghosts don't make footsteps, and vibes don't either, Julie told herself. Maybe the Ogilvies had come back? She left the radio off and decided to go up and ask if they had been there the previous night.

Out in the hallway she climbed the stairs. The door to the apartment above her own was closed. She knocked—and stepped back in surprise as the force of her knock pushed the door open.

"Hello?" Julie called. But there was no answer.

She hesitated, feeling like Goldilocks at the

three bears' door, debating whether to enter an empty home. She looked tentatively into the living room of the apartment, wrinkling her nose at the lingering smell of stale cigarette smoke. The room was completely deserted. No furniture at all, no rug on the bare wooden floor, no curtains at the window. She reached out and pulled the door shut, wondering why it was unlocked.

Julie headed back down the stairs and then stopped suddenly as she heard the soft tread of footsteps above her. Someone *was* in that empty apartment!

She tiptoed back up and then hesitated, her hand on the doorknob.

Suddenly the knob turned under her hand. Julie jumped. Someone was on the other side of the door.

4
TROUBLE WITH A CAPITAL T

Julie stifled a scream and hurtled back down the stairs. Someone was in there, but *who*? She hadn't seen anyone. *Could* there be a ghost?

Of course not, Julie assured herself. Maybe the Ogilvies had sent a housecleaner, as Mom had suggested. But then why was there no sign of a vacuum or a bucket and mop? And why would someone cleaning the place *hide* when Julie entered? The idea that someone was hiding seemed even more frightening than the possibility of there being a ghost.

Calm down, Julie told herself firmly. She slipped back inside her own apartment and shut the door. *There's a simple explanation—figure it out.*

Well, who else had a key to the apartment? The landlords, of course—but the Vernons were out of town, and why would they hide? Same with the Ogilvies, who obviously had already moved out. They too had no need to hide. And Maggie's parents wouldn't get their key till next month. But maybe the Ogilvies had left their door unlocked when they'd moved out, and some neighborhood kids had come in to mess around? Maybe they were playing up there now and had hidden when they heard Julie come in.

That theory made the most sense, and Julie felt better. But she waited just inside her apartment door, cracking it open to peek out so that she could see if anyone came downstairs. Time dragged, and nobody came. Just when she was about to give up and get back to her quilt square, she heard footsteps.

They were not the sounds of someone hurrying down the steps in a normal way but rather the slow, cautious steps of someone descending stealthily. Julie held her breath, peeking through the crack of the open apartment door as a pair of feet in battered black high-tops came into view, and then blue jeans and a green sweatshirt. *T. J.!*

"What are *you* doing here?" shrieked Julie.

"Shh," T. J. hissed. He looked haggard and worried.

"Are you okay?" She held her apartment door open for him. "Want to come in?"

He shook his head, eyes shadowed.

"Look, I could tell at school that something was bugging you," she pressed. "Will you please tell me what's going on? Maybe I can help."

T. J. chewed his lip. "I'm in big trouble. I wish you could help, but it's my own fault, and there's nothing you can do."

"I could *try*," Julie offered.

"Come upstairs," he said with a heavy sigh, "and I'll show you."

Upstairs? Julie couldn't imagine what he wanted to show her, but she followed him as he turned and trudged up to the Ogilvies' apartment. She gasped when he pulled a key out of his jacket pocket.

"It was *you* in here!" cried Julie. "You scared me to death."

"I didn't mean for anyone to hear me,"

he said, flushing. "I was trying to be quiet. But I guess empty apartments echo. Or maybe the sound gets carried through the heating vents." He shrugged. "Anyway, when I heard somebody coming, I hid. I didn't know it was you."

"But—what's wrong?" demanded Julie, stepping cautiously into the apartment. They shouldn't be in here, Julie knew. They were trespassing. It felt very strange.

T. J. furrowed his brow and led her through the empty living room, into the small bedroom. "Oh, Julie," he said, his voice anguished, "I've done a terrible thing."

He put his hand on the knob of the closet door. Julie could see that his hand was shaking.

"Tell me," she whispered.

T. J. jerked open the closet door. A shaft of waning sunlight from the window fell across a guitar. A shiny silver guitar.

Julie opened her mouth in surprise. "But— but isn't that—?"

"Yep," sighed T. J. "Mr. Vernon's pride and joy."

Gingerly, Julie pulled the guitar out of the

closet and sank to the floor with it in her lap. She ran her hand over the silver surface, and flakes of paint came off on her skin. She traced her fingers down two long cracks at the base of the neck. "Oh *no*. What happened, T. J.?"

He glanced at the guitar, and then away, as if the sight of it pained him. Crossing to the bedroom window, he leaned on the sill, his back to her. "It happened when I went to feed the Vernons' cat that first time."

He whirled around, and she saw the distress in his eyes. His cheeks were flushed.

"I let myself in with the key they'd given me. I went to the kitchen and mixed the special food. That cat eats like a king. Real chicken from their fridge, shredded up and mixed with vitamin oil. And I filled his bowl with fresh water. He started gobbling up his food, and I should have left right then—I mean, I'd done what I was supposed to do, right?"

T. J. scrubbed his fingers through his hair, making it stand wildly on end. "But I didn't leave. Nope, I just *had* to go look at Mr. Vernon's guitar collection. I just wanted one quick look. I wasn't going to touch anything—just *look*."

"Oh, no . . ." Julie could see where this story was heading.

"Oh, *yes*," T. J. moaned. "So I went into the library . . ." His voice trailed off. He crossed the room and collapsed next to Julie on the floor.

"I just wanted to hold it," he whispered. "Danny Kendricks's guitar." He reached out and stroked the gleaming silver guitar with one trembling hand. "He was left-handed, like me! I just wanted to put my fingers on the strings and feel what *he* felt."

Julie nodded sympathetically.

T. J. sighed. "I had to stand on a chair to reach," he continued. "And while I was standing on it, the cat came slinking into the room. He jumped up on top of a display cabinet, and then up onto the mantel. And right when I was lifting the guitar down from the wall, Mister Precious leaped onto me—right from the mantel! His claws dug into my shoulder, and I fell off the chair and . . . oh, Julie, *I dropped the guitar*." His eyes filled with tears, and he dashed them away with his fist. "I wanted to tell you about it at school today, but other kids were always around. Look at it! I don't know what I'm going to do. Mr. Vernon will kill me."

"Oh, T. J." Julie wasn't sure how to comfort her friend. Mr. Vernon wouldn't kill T. J., of course. But Danny Kendricks's silver Stratocaster was valuable—and irreplaceable.

"Was Jasper home when this happened?" Julie asked. "Did he see you with the guitar?"

"No, I don't think so," said T. J. "His car wasn't in the driveway when I got there. The only other people around were the photographers, and they were in another room on the other side of the house taking more photos for the catalogue. I don't think anyone saw me take it."

The dusting of silver paint on her hand shimmered. The weight of T. J.'s despair made her feel slightly dizzy. "But why did you bring it here?" Julie asked quietly. "And how did you get the key to this apartment?"

"*You* gave me the idea," T. J. murmured.

"*Me*? You're blaming me for this mess?"

"Shh! Of course I'm not blaming you. But you mentioned that the Vernons owned your apartment building, and you said there was an empty apartment above yours. I remembered you saying that Maggie's family wasn't moving in until next month. So I grabbed the big ring of keys that Mr. Vernon keeps in his home office, labeled for all the real estate properties he owns. I'd seen the keys earlier when Mr. Vernon gave me their house key, before they left on their trip."

T. J. stood up again and started pacing the empty room, his face anguished. "I couldn't put the guitar back up on the wall because I was worried I'd make the break worse. But I also couldn't just leave it on the floor because Jasper might find it when he got home—"

"So you brought it here last night!" Julie exclaimed. "It was *you* making all that racket!" She breathed a sigh of relief.

T. J. looked confused. "I wasn't here last night."

Julie's heart jumped. "But if it wasn't you making those thumps, then who *was* it?"

T. J. shrugged. "I don't know what you're talking about," he said. "Aren't you listening, Julie? I didn't want to leave the guitar at the Vernons' house, where Jasper might find it, and I couldn't take it home with me, where my parents would see what I'd done. I knew from what you'd said that this apartment was empty. So I hid the guitar in the broom closet at the Vernons' just for last night—and then I went straight back after school today. As soon as I fed the cat, I wrapped the guitar in a blanket and brought it here."

"T. J., that's stealing—" Julie began, but he cut her off.

"No it's not, because Mr. Vernon owns this building, so the guitar is still on his property."

Julie looked around the empty room and shivered. She was starting to understand what the Ogilvies had meant when they said the apartment had bad vibes. "Well, I don't think you should keep the guitar here," she said. "What if a cleaning crew comes in and finds it, or painters—or whoever was in here making all that racket last night?" Just the mention of the ghostly bumps and thumps made her skin creep. "In fact, we really shouldn't be in here at all. We're trespassing."

"Keep the guitar for me," he begged. "Please? Just till I figure out what to do next."

Julie fingered the guitar's broken neck. The sight of the cracks made her feel queasy. "Maybe instead you should take it home and tell your parents—and the Vernons. They'll understand it was an accident."

"*No!*" gasped T. J. "I want to fix it before I tell anyone! I've *got* to fix it."

He showed her some wood glue he'd brought from home, hoping he could mend the crack somehow.

Julie eyed the glue bottle. "Well, I'm not sure you should try to fix it yourself," she told T. J. "What if you make it worse?"

"I have to fix it—I'm going to be in so much trouble! I think we should at least try."

Julie didn't like the sound of "we." She had no idea how to repair a guitar. But she knew a broken guitar could never be sold at the auction, even if it had belonged to Danny Kendricks. All that money it would have brought in for the seabirds—lost! And poor T. J.—she could understand how awful he felt, damaging something so unique and valuable.

Then she had an idea. "There's a music shop on Haight Street," she said slowly. "They have tons of guitars in the window. What if we take the guitar there? Maybe they can fix it, or at least know of someone who can."

T. J. brightened for a moment but then slumped again. "I hope I can afford repairs— all I have is what I've saved up from my paper route, and that was supposed to go toward my own new guitar." He looked ready to cry.

Julie reluctantly agreed to keep the guitar hidden at the back of her closet until they went to the guitar shop. "I'll go with you to the music store tomorrow right after school," she promised. "But if they can't fix it—or if you can't afford it—you *have* to tell the Vernons."

He sighed. "I will," he said. "I guess . . . I guess I'll have no choice."

5
A MUSICAL MYSTERY

That night Julie tossed and turned, her sleep broken by confusing dreams of pelicans, ghosts, and guitars.

She arrived at school late because she'd left her lunch in its brown paper sack on the kitchen counter and had to run back half a block to get it. Fortunately Mrs. Duncan was busy handing out squares of white cloth and didn't seem to notice when Julie slipped into her seat just after the bell rang. T. J. turned around in his seat and gave her a small wave. He, too, looked as if he hadn't slept well.

"This cotton square will be your canvas," the teacher told the class, holding up one of the neatly cut panels. "Sewn together, your squares will make a quilt for the auction. I hope you've all been working on sketches that can be transferred to the fabric—and then filled in with fabric paint or decorated with patchwork or simple embroidery."

Julie focused on tracing her sketch of the pelican wearing sunglasses onto the fabric. She added a jaunty hat. She found if she concentrated very hard, she could stop worrying about the broken guitar for a little while.

But after school, as Julie and T. J. walked to her apartment, the guitar was heavy on their minds. "If only I hadn't tried to hold it," T. J. muttered.

"T. J., you didn't mean to drop it," Julie pointed out.

But T. J. wouldn't be comforted. "If only that cat had stayed on the floor where cats belong!"

Of course, Julie realized, *it's easier for him if it's Mister Precious's fault.* "Well," she said, "let's hope the people at the music store know how to fix it."

"Yeah." T.J groaned. "But if they can't, I'll be grounded until I'm about ninety."

They retrieved the broken guitar from Julie's closet, wrapped it up in a yellow blanket, and carried it several blocks to the music store. Julie felt as if she were carrying a big baby, swaddled against the spring wind.

A sign on the door read "Help Wanted," and a buzzer sounded as they entered. Julie and T. J. stepped into a cacophony of sound with rock music pulsing in the background and customers trying out different instruments they might want to buy. A curly-haired boy of about twelve strummed chords on a red electric guitar. A girl Tracy's age in a long peasant skirt held a violin to her chin and practiced her scales. A little boy thumped on a large kettledrum while his mother stood by, shaking her head. Julie winced at the noise, but T. J. gazed rapturously at all the guitars hanging on the walls. "Wow," he said, eyes wide. "I'm in heaven."

"Hey there," the bearded young man behind the counter greeted them. "How may I help you?" He raised his eyebrows at the yellow bundle they laid carefully on the countertop.

"Um, do you fix guitars?" asked Julie.

"Sure do, kiddo. Simple things right here in the shop, while you wait. Bigger jobs get sent out to the experts." He leaned toward them with a smile. "Did you pop a string?"

"Worse than that," mumbled T. J.

"This was once Danny Kendricks's guitar," Julie clarified, "but now it belongs to a friend of ours."

The curly-haired boy who had been testing the red guitar leaned on the counter. "Did I hear somebody say *Danny Kendricks*?" the boy asked, his expression eager. "Kendricks was my hero! I'm practicing one of his riffs now—listen to this!" He started plucking at the red guitar, his eyes half-closed with concentration.

"Hey, Matt," interrupted the clerk. "Not now, buddy. I'm waiting on customers here."

"Sorry, man," said the boy, flushing slightly. He unslung the red guitar from around his neck and handed it to the clerk. Then he reached behind the sales counter for his skateboard and headed for the door. "See you later."

"Thanks for your help today, Matt," the clerk called before the door closed behind the boy. The clerk shook his head. "We can't give him a job because he's too young, but he helps me out—getting instruments off the wall for customers to try—and in return we let him practice. He hangs out here a lot." The clerk returned the red guitar to its stand next to the wall, and then turned back and laid his hands gently on the yellow blanket. "So is this really Danny Kendricks's guitar? Well, let's see it."

Julie unwrapped it carefully as T. J. explained in a low voice how he'd dropped it.

"What a bummer," the clerk said. He stared in awe at the cracked silver guitar. "This was his guitar—for real? Far out! I saw Kendricks in concert—twice."

"We're hoping you can fix it," Julie said.

The clerk didn't seem to be listening. He was running his hands over the instrument with reverence. "Oh, man, this is devastating," he lamented. "Like, a *serious* drag."

"I know," said T. J. "Believe me, I *know*.

No need to rub it in."

"But can you help us?" Julie pressed.

The clerk shook his shaggy head mournfully. "Well, no, not me, myself. But our manager knows everything there is to know about guitars, so I'll just call him to come and look at the damage. He'll know what to do." He walked around the counter and headed toward the back of the shop.

Other customers were beginning to line up behind Julie and T. J. at the counter, craning their necks to see what the problem was. Julie tucked the yellow blanket protectively back around the guitar. She didn't like people staring.

"It's kind of like a car crash on the freeway, with people trying to see the wreckage," Julie whispered to T. J.

"I can help you over at this cash register," chirped a girl in a tie-dyed T-shirt. Julie felt grateful to her as the line of people moved over to her station. Just then their clerk came striding back to the sales counter with a bespectacled man at his side.

"I'm Mr. Hammond, the manager," the older man said, raising his voice over the din of musical instruments. "Gary tells me you need some help with a Danny Kendricks guitar—can that be correct?"

"Yes, it is," said T. J. gratefully.

Mr. Hammond looked eagerly at the yellow bundle. "May I see it, please?"

"We need to get it repaired—fast," Julie told him, unwrapping the blanket again. "It's supposed to be sold at a benefit auction in two weeks."

"I see." The manager pursed his lips, lifting the guitar carefully to inspect it from another angle. "Danny Kendricks," he said. "One of the finest guitar players I have ever heard. Such a tragedy when he died. I met him myself, once. He came right into this shop about three or four years ago—" Abruptly he broke off, frowning. Then he shook his head and snorted.

"Well, well," he said, laying the guitar on the blanket. He glared at Julie and T. J. "That's a silly trick."

Julie and T. J. looked at each other blankly. "What trick?" asked T. J.

"You almost had me fooled." Mr. Hammond scowled at them. "Not for long, though."

"What do you mean?" Julie asked. "Can't the guitar be fixed?"

"No point, is there?" Mr. Hammond replied. The clerk looked from his manager to Julie and T. J., and then back again, as if watching a tennis match.

Mr. Hammond pointedly turned away to answer a customer's question. Julie and T. J. waited, perplexed. Then Mr. Hammond turned back to them, frowning fiercely. "Don't waste my time, kids."

"What?" Julie bit her lip. "You mean the guitar can't be fixed after all?"

"Oh, one of our repairmen can probably fix your guitar, but why bother?"

"Why *bother*?" T. J. sounded outraged.

"You might as well use glue and patch it up yourselves. Save your money—and everybody's time. You know perfectly well this isn't going to fetch any real money at an auction." He shoved the guitar at T. J. with none of the reverence he'd shown when he first handled it. "We're busy here and we've got other customers."

"But this is Danny Kendricks's guitar," Julie pleaded. "And we've *got* to get it fixed—"

"I don't know what you're trying to pull, but this *isn't* Kendricks's guitar," Mr. Hammond said flatly. "It's not even a real Fender Stratocaster. It's just a cheap fake!"

A CLEVER COUNTERFEIT

Shocked, Julie stared at the manager. Then she turned to T. J. "A *fake*?"

The bearded clerk, Gary, was nodding now, as if he'd suspected as much.

"That's impossible!" protested T. J. "Mr. Vernon—he's the owner—told me it's one of the best pieces in his whole collection."

Mr. Hammond shook his head. "You mean you really didn't know? Then I'm sorry. But the guitar is basically a piece of junk. Not even a very good copy, when you look closely."

"But how could that be? Mr. Vernon got it from Danny Kendricks himself!" said Julie.

"Yeah," Gary snorted. "And my mom's the Queen of England."

Mr. Hammond shrugged. "I highly doubt

this belonged to Danny Kendricks. It's just a cheap knockoff. Nothing special."

"No, look—it has to be a Fender Stratocaster," T. J. said, sounding desperate. "See? It says so right here."

"That's just a stick-on label," Mr. Hammond replied. "And look at these strings: Kendricks was left-handed, but he played a right-handed guitar—upside down—and restrung the strings. This guitar is strung properly for a right-handed player." He sighed. "This is just a cheap imitation of a Strat. We don't even sell such inferior instruments. See here—the paint is flaking off."

Julie looked carefully. She saw that the scratch marks Mr. Vernon had proudly pointed out to them, the marks Danny Kendricks had made while playing his famous wild solos, were gone. Had someone painted over them? But why?

"At least you don't have to be worried that you've wrecked a fine piece of rock and roll history," the manager said less severely.

T. J. and Julie looked at each other, puzzled. "Then . . . I guess there's no problem," said T. J., breaking into a relieved grin. He took the blanket-wrapped guitar into his arms. "What a load off my mind! Thanks!"

The buzzer sounded again as they left. The door closed behind them, shutting out the layers of music. T. J. turned to grin at Julie. "I'm off the hook!"

She nodded with a hesitant smile. It *was* a relief to know he had not ruined a valuable guitar.

But what had happened between the last auction, when Mr. Vernon had proudly shown them Danny Kendricks's guitar, and when T. J. had dropped the cheap replica? Had someone tampered with the strings and paint on the guitar Mr. Vernon had shown them? Or were there two guitars? Neither explanation made sense.

She was distracted from these thoughts by the sight of a couple walking along the other side of the street. She recognized her former neighbors, the Ogilvies. Julie waved casually but clutched T. J.'s arm with her other hand. "Those are the people who just moved out of the apartment upstairs," she whispered to him.

"Think what they'd say if they knew we'd been in there!"

Across the street, Mrs. Ogilvie raised her hand, acknowledging Julie.

Just then a skateboarder wearing his black baseball cap backward whooshed by them on his skateboard, and T. J. nimbly dodged out of his way. The boy waved, and they saw it was Matt, the curly-haired boy who liked to help out in the music shop. As T. J. raised his hand to wave back, the blanket started slipping off the guitar, exposing its smooth silver body. He and Julie smoothed it back into place. "Can we keep this in your closet?" T. J. asked Julie. "Just for now?"

"I guess so. And we can get a snack—I'm hungry," she said, watching as Matt rode his skateboard across the street. He jumped over the curb, landing recklessly right in front of the Ogilvies, who stopped just in time to avoid a collision.

Show-off! thought Julie. She and T. J. hurried around the corner and up the street. They peeked into the storefront window of Gladrags.

Julie's mom had her back turned. They ducked and ran past the window so that they wouldn't get caught with the yellow bundle.

"Phew—we made it!" T. J. said, wiping his forehead. They climbed the stairs to Julie's apartment and went straight to her bedroom. After they stowed the blanket-wrapped guitar in the back of her closet, Julie led the way into her kitchen and opened the cupboard. She handed T. J. a package of chocolate chip cookies. As he sprawled in a chair at the table, still grinning in relief about the fake guitar, Julie heated milk in a pan for their cocoa. He chomped cookies and talked with his mouth full, his cheerful chatter filling the room.

Julie stirred cocoa powder and sugar into the milk and whisked it to a froth, then poured it into two mugs, set them on the table, and sat down to think. Her head was swimming with all the new information they had learned at the music shop.

"You know," she said slowly, "it *is* a relief that you didn't break Kendricks's guitar. But at the same time, it's not really good news that the guitar is a fake."

"What do you mean?" T. J. asked through a mouthful of cookie. "It's *great* news that I haven't wrecked Danny Kendricks's guitar! The Vernons will be relieved, too. And I won't have to spend the rest of my life trying to earn enough money to replace a priceless Strat!" Nothing could dampen T. J.'s elation.

"That's true," said Julie. She sipped her hot cocoa, swallowing carefully. "But think about it. I'm positive Mr. Vernon showed us a different guitar. That guitar was strung left-handed, and it had those scratches on it, remember? And I just can't believe Mr. Vernon would mistake a fake guitar for a real one—I mean, he's a collector, and it was his favorite guitar in his whole collection." She paused and blew on her cocoa, frowning with concentration. "But if *that* guitar was the real thing, that means someone had to replace the real one with the fake."

"Well," said T. J., "it's possible Mr. Vernon switched the guitars himself. Maybe he sold the real one to someone and just stuck the fake in its place so that the display wouldn't look unbalanced." T. J. seemed quite pleased with his explanation.

"But they left for their trip the very next day," said Julie. "And besides, Mr. Vernon said he wanted to sell the guitar at the next auction to help the seabirds."

"Actually," T. J. corrected her, "it's his *wife* who wants him to auction Kendricks's guitar. I had the feeling Mr. Vernon would rather keep it in his collection. Maybe she switched it so that her husband could keep the real guitar and they could auction off the fake one instead."

"But Mrs. Vernon is a really nice person. She's *friends* with my mom," Julie protested. "I can't believe Mrs. Vernon would try to auction off a fake guitar! She's not that kind of person."

"Well," allowed T. J., "then maybe she doesn't know it's a fake. Maybe *Mrs.* Vernon isn't that kind of person, but we don't really know *Mr.* Vernon very well, do we? Maybe *he is* that kind of person."

Julie thought about this for a moment.

"So are you saying that when Mrs. Vernon asked him to sell the guitar at the auction, he decided he just couldn't bear to part with it after all, so he had a fake one made—like a decoy—and hung it on the wall in place of the real one before they left on their business trip?"

"Right," said T. J. "That way he's keeping the real one safely hidden away somewhere so that it won't get sold at the auction."

Julie paused, considering T. J.'s theory. "You could be right," she finally said. "Except I think that anybody who is really into guitars would spot the fake at the auction, and then Mr. Vernon would get caught trying to pull off a scam."

Now T. J. became quiet. After a moment Julie said slowly, "I guess whoever put the decoy there is someone who isn't worried about the fake being spotted—because by then he'd have made his escape with the *real* guitar, the valuable one. Which would mean—" She stared at T. J. with round eyes.

"What? What would it mean?" asked T. J., frowning.

"It would mean that someone *else*—a *thief*—took the real one and replaced it with the fake. And the Vernons don't know."

T. J. cupped his hands around his mug. "That's a creepy thought," he said. "I mean, who could have stolen the guitar without the Vernons knowing it? And when?"

Julie stared out the kitchen window at the darkening day. Wisps of evening fog off the bay hovered above the buildings like ghosts. "I wonder if the nosy neighbor you mentioned saw anything," she wondered aloud. "What was her name?"

"Mrs. Buzbee," said T. J. "The Vernons said she's always snooping around and prying, and then trying to explain herself by saying she's seen an intruder or something. But what if she really *did* see an intruder? Or what if—" he broke off. "Julie, maybe *she's* the thief!"

"I suppose she could be," Julie said. "After all, Mrs. Buzbee would know when she could sneak in because she always knows when the Vernons are home and when they're away.

And she knows about Mr. Vernon's valuable collections."

"But it's still kind of weird," T. J. said. "I mean, a *regular* thief would just take the guitar and leave quickly. What kind of thief brings a *replacement* guitar and carefully hangs it on the wall after taking the real one?"

Julie frowned. "What kind of thief?" she repeated slowly. "Well, somebody trying to fool people, I guess." Was Mrs. Buzbee that sort of thief? "Too bad Ms. Knight isn't around," Julie said. "The housekeeper would know of any visitors to the house recently. Somebody at the auction, maybe. You know, somebody who might have had the opportunity . . ." Her voice trailed off as a terrible thought struck her. "T. J.," she whispered, *"you* had the opportunity. The Vernons might think you took it yourself!"

T. J. stared at her, his eyes round and worried. "Let's track the housekeeper down," he said grimly. "She may have seen something. Or—wait! She could even be the thief herself! I mean, think about it. Usually in a mystery, the butler did it. A housekeeper is sort of the same thing as a butler."

Julie nodded. It was true, the housekeeper would have plenty of opportunity to substitute a fake guitar for the real Fender Stratocaster. She might want more money than she earned working for the Vernons. She might have devised a plan to steal the real guitar and sell it, and planted the decoy to delay the discovery that the real guitar was missing. "And Ms. Knight isn't the sort of housekeeper you read about in books," Julie added. "You know—the kind who's been with the family for years and years and is dedicated to them. Mrs. Vernon said Ms. Knight is a student just taking a year off from college, working to earn money for acting lessons in Hollywood."

It felt good to have a plan of action. They needed to find the thief so that everyone would know T. J. was innocent. Then Julie thought of someone else who needed money. "What about that nephew?"

He just wants money to appear in his pockets,

Mrs. Vernon had said about their nephew at the auction. What if the nephew had stolen the guitar and sold it for cash—and put the fake one on the wall so that his uncle wouldn't know?

"Jasper." T. J. nodded. "Mrs. Vernon said he won't even pry himself off the couch to try to find a job." T. J. looked at his watch. "But speaking of jobs, I'd better go. It's nearly time to feed Mister Precious."

"I'll see if I can come with you," Julie said. "We can at least talk to Mrs. Buzbee and try to find the housekeeper." She paused. "You know, we could tell my mom about this. After all, she knows Mrs. Vernon really well, and she could explain what happened—"

"No, don't say anything yet," T. J. begged. "Maybe it's just . . . well, some sort of mix-up. We have until the Vernons get back to try to figure things out."

"Okay," Julie agreed. She drank the last of her cocoa and carried their mugs to the sink.

They went down the back staircase and found Julie's mother behind the counter in

Gladrags. But when Julie explained about T. J.'s cat-sitting job and asked to go with him, Mom shook her head.

"No, honey. It'll be dark soon—"

"But Mom," Julie interrupted, "I'm almost eleven. I'll be fine."

"It's almost time for dinner," Mom said. "I'm just closing up here. Why don't you go tomorrow right after school, and I'll send Tracy to pick you up to bring you home again?"

"Well, okay," Julie said. "Tomorrow, then. All right, T. J.?"

"Yeah, sure," he agreed. But he didn't look happy about going alone, and Julie knew why. She found it unsettling enough to have a fake guitar hidden in her closet; the thought of meeting up with the Vernons' nephew or housekeeper or nosy neighbor—any of whom might be a thief—was even more unsettling.

"T. J.," she called as she saw him out the door, into the darkening street, "be careful."

7

AT THE VERNON MANSION

Right after school the following day, Julie and T. J. caught a bus to the foot of Nob Hill. "It was weird yesterday," T. J. said as the bus set off in the busy afternoon traffic. "The whole time I was heading to the Vernons', I felt spooked—as if someone was watching me."

"Watching you from *where*?" she asked, eyes widening.

He shrugged. "I don't know. I just felt ... *watched*. But I didn't see anybody I recognized, other than that kid we met at the music store— you know, Matt? He was on his skateboard by the bus stop near Gladrags. While we were waiting for the bus, he showed me how to grind the curb! He's really good."

"Was there anybody at the Vernons' house

when you got there?" Julie asked.

"Nope. Just my good buddy, Mister Precious."

The bus let them off, and they hiked up the steep sidewalk to the Vernons' imposing residence. A low-slung green sports car was parked in front. "Looks like Jasper is home this time," said T. J. "Mr. Vernon said Jasper gets to use the Alfa Romeo whenever he wants." His eyes gleamed with appreciation. "Lucky guy! It's a *beauty*."

Even Julie, who wasn't especially interested in cars, liked the look of the sleek and shiny green car. She brushed the four-leaf clover emblem with her fingertips as she passed. How Tracy would love to drive it!

They knocked on the front door. When Jasper didn't appear, they knocked again, and then pressed the old-fashioned buzzer that served as a doorbell. Still getting no response, T. J. finally used the key Mrs. Vernon had given him. The door swung open, and Julie and T. J. stepped into the spacious marble hallway.

"Hello? Jasper?" T. J. called.

There was no answer. T. J. and Julie glanced at each other, then closed the front door behind them and headed down the grand hallway, peering into the elegant living room and dining room as they passed. "Maybe he's upstairs somewhere," said Julie.

"Maybe," T. J. replied. "Well, let's go feed the cat." He led the way to the back of the house.

As they passed the closed library door, they could hear muffled laughter.

"Jasper?" T. J. called again. He knocked on the door. The laughter stopped immediately.

"Who's there?" Jasper barked.

T. J. opened the door, and there was Jasper, lolling on the couch with a box of tissues at his side. The TV was tuned in to a movie—a Western. Gunslingers were shooting in a saloon.

"Hi," said T. J. "I'm just here to feed the cat. Um . . . this is Julie," he added as she stepped into the room behind him.

The library was a mess. Wadded tissues lay on the floor. Dirty dishes were stacked on the glass cabinet where Mr. Vernon's antique watch collection was displayed.

"Hey there, T. J. and friend," Jasper greeted them casually. His voice was thick and husky. "Good thing you're here now, kids. You can make me some dinner."

"I'm just here to feed the cat," T. J. repeated.

Jasper peered up at Julie. "Well then, little girlfriend, how about *you* bring me a hot drink and make me a sandwich while you're at it." He snapped his fingers at her and grinned. "Make it double-quick, 'cause I'm starving."

Julie put her hands on her hips. "I'm not your girlfriend," she said indignantly, "and we're not your servants!"

Jasper laughed. "Well, go on then, feed the demon cat, and split. But just don't let that cat out of the kitchen, whatever you do! It took me half an hour to lock him up in the laundry room last night."

"Mister Precious isn't supposed to be locked up," T. J. said reprovingly, but Julie saw he was looking with anxious eyes at the empty space on the wall behind the couch where the guitar had been displayed. She lowered her own gaze and looked at other things instead. The empty pizza box on the coffee table. The glass dome holding Abraham Lincoln's big black top hat. The big windows looking out into the back garden. The long curtains stirred as if blown by a breeze, and in a sudden shaft of sunlight, the air was full of dust motes, and the antique top hat didn't look rusty at all, but velvety black.

"You'd better get going, before you catch whatever I have." Jasper coughed into another tissue. "I'm probably contagious." Julie noticed that Jasper hadn't mentioned the guitar. Did that mean he was so under the weather that he had come in and flopped onto the couch without noticing the instrument was missing? *Or does he know full well that it's missing?* she wondered.

The curtains stirred again. This time Julie bit back a gasp as a realization hit her: *the windows were not open.*

Her heart thudding, Julie forced a friendly smile on her face. "On second thought, I can make you that sandwich while T. J. feeds the cat," she said brightly. She took T. J.'s arm and pulled him toward the kitchen.

"He should get his own food—we're not his servants," T. J. sputtered, but Julie closed the door to the kitchen and leaned toward him.

"Someone is in there with him," she hissed.

His eyes widened. "What? Where?"

"Hiding behind the curtain. I'm almost sure of it!"

T. J. looked alarmed. "Do you think we interrupted him and somebody else trying to steal more things?"

"I don't know," Julie whispered, "but let's hurry and get out of here." The memory of the shifting brocade curtains made the back of Julie's neck prickle.

They let Mister Precious out of the laundry room. Haughtily, the fluffy cat stalked past them and leaped up onto the kitchen table. T. J. opened the refrigerator and took out a covered bowl of cooked chicken. Quickly he shredded it and added a little milk and the various supplements as Mrs. Vernon had directed. Julie slapped some peanut butter and strawberry jam between two slices of bread. She poured Jasper a glass of orange juice and carried it, along with the sandwich, back into the library.

Jasper took the food and grinned. "Thanks. This'll be fine. I'll tell Aunt Eleanor to hire you, whenever you want a full-time job."

Julie couldn't help glancing at the long curtains. This time they didn't move at all, but it seemed to her that the closet door was slightly ajar now. Hadn't it been fully closed before? She felt like running out of the room but forced herself to stay calm. "Okay, we're leaving now."

"Ta-ta," Jasper said airily, lying back on the couch and propping his feet on the arm. "Oh, would you turn up the volume a little for me?"

Julie pretended she hadn't heard him and closed the door to the library quickly behind her. She darted down the hall to where T. J. was waiting by the front door. Mister Precious stood at the top of the grand staircase, meowing down at them. The many unknown rooms upstairs could be filled with any number of intruders.

"Let's get out of here!" She couldn't leave the mansion fast enough.

T. J. pulled the front door open, and they hurried outside. He locked it again behind them. "That guy makes me mad."

"Me, too." Julie glanced over her shoulder and then looked at her watch. Her sister would be arriving soon to drive her home.

"Look, there's that Mrs. Buzbee," T. J. said.

A small, round woman with gray hair arranged in tight curls was standing at her front door across the street, watching them. Her face was wreathed in a smile, and she raised her arm to wave at them. *She doesn't look at all like a thief*, Julie thought. But then she sighed. Of course, any good thief would be careful not to look like one.

"Let's go talk to her," Julie suggested. "Maybe she saw whether Jasper went into the house alone—or not."

Mrs. Buzbee smiled eagerly as Julie and T. J. crossed the street. "Now what's going on *here*?" she greeted them. "What's happening? Who are you young people?"

"T. J. just came to feed the cat," Julie told her. "I'm Julie Albright. I'm helping."

"So, you're the kitty-sitters while Ms. Knight is away, eh?" Mrs. Buzbee said. "Well, I daresay it's a good way to earn some pocket money." The old lady nodded, her eyes bright with interest. "Seems to me that nephew should be helping out, if you ask me!" she added in her raspy voice. "But he won't stay home long enough to be of any help. Always racing around. Drives too fast! He'll do himself harm one of these days."

"Well, he's home safe enough now," Julie said. "Lying down with a bad cold—in the library." She watched Mrs. Buzbee's expression. Did she imagine it, or did the woman flinch slightly when Julie said the name of the room? If Mrs. Buzbee was guilty of taking the real silver guitar and leaving the fake behind, she might be worried that anybody hanging out in that room would notice something different about the guitar on the wall.

But the neighbor's expression gave nothing away. "Oh, *sick*, did he say? That's funny, because he was just coming around with a friend less than an hour ago," the woman said. "Always in and out at all hours of the day and night! That young man should get a job, that's what I say, and I told him that to his face. And do you know what he said?" She pursed her lips disapprovingly. "He said he only wanted money if he didn't have to lift a finger to get it. Imagine, admitting that right out! Have you ever heard of anything more shameful? Bone lazy!"

Julie kept her voice casual. "It's nice that his friend can take care of him, since he's sick."

"Well, he didn't look the least bit sick roaring up in that car with his girlfriend. But yes, I suppose the girl could play nurse if she had a mind to," Mrs. Buzbee said.

So there *was* someone with Jasper. Julie and T. J. exchanged a troubled look. Why had he hidden his girlfriend behind the curtains if she wasn't an accomplice? Were they inside right now, stealing other things from Mr. Vernon's collections?

"So Mister Precious is all right, then, is he?"

Mrs. Buzbee asked, her eyes sharp. "Didn't cause you any trouble, then?"

T. J. cleared his throat. "No," he said. "The cat's fine. Um . . . we wondered, though, when the housekeeper will be back. We thought you might know."

Mrs. Buzbee looked disappointed. "I wish I did know! I'd feel better having Louisa at the house. That Jasper! He might take it into his head to throw a wild party while his aunt and uncle are gone." She added darkly, "It's happened before."

"Ms. Knight is visiting her mother in the hospital," Julie said, trying to draw the conversation back to the housekeeper's whereabouts. "Do you know which hospital?"

"I'm sorry to say I don't." Mrs. Buzbee looked disheartened not to know that piece of information. Then she brightened. "But I do know where Louisa's older sister lives. Louisa visits her big sister on weekends, you see. Tullie, her name is. Stands for Tallulah. She'd know which hospital their mother is in, of course."

"Oh, thank you," said Julie. "Do you have her phone number?"

"No, but I have her address because I drove Louisa to see her sister once when her car wasn't working. Hold on, and I'll write it down for you." Mrs. Buzbee went into her house.

"I think it was Jasper who took the guitar," said T. J. as he and Julie waited. "He's got his girlfriend or somebody in there with him, and there was no reason to hide her—unless they were up to no good."

"I think so, too," agreed Julie. "But we should still talk to Ms. Knight and ask her if anyone suspicious has been to the house lately. Jasper could be selling his aunt and uncle's valuable things right there at the house."

"But I don't want to tell her why we're asking," said T. J. "I don't want anyone to know I broke the guitar until I tell the Vernons myself."

"We'll find a way to ask without telling her why we want to know," said Julie. "I'll ask Tracy if she can take us there right now. She can take you home afterward."

She stopped talking abruptly as Mrs. Buzbee returned.

"Here you are," she said, handing Julie a slip of paper. "It's off Market Street. Now you say hello to Tullie for me when you see her."

As a car pulled up to the curb, Julie and T. J. said good-bye to Mrs. Buzbee, who was peering inquisitively at Tracy in the driver's seat.

"Will you drop us off on Market Street?" Julie asked her sister as she climbed into the backseat so that T. J. could sit up front. "Pretty please? We can walk home from there."

Tracy glanced at the address on the paper Julie was waving. "Sure, I suppose so."

As the car set off down the street, Julie glanced back over her shoulder out the rear window. She saw the neighbor quickly cross the Vernons' driveway.

"Look, T. J.!" Julie cried. "Mrs. Buzbee's sneaking a peek in the Vernons' windows!"

8
SUSPECTS AND SHADOWS

T. J. and Julie craned their necks as Tracy pulled away from the curb. Then Julie saw a figure detach itself from the wall of the Vernons' house. She glimpsed a black baseball cap—it was Matt, the boy with the skateboard. He stood staring after the car, then jumped on his skateboard and started down the steep street.

Julie sat back in the seat as her sister reached the bottom of the hill and navigated the turn. "Did you see that?" Julie asked T. J.

He nodded. "I'm sure glad Mrs. Buzbee isn't *my* neighbor," he said.

"Me, too. But I meant the boy. Matt."

"Matt?" said T. J. "What was he doing there?"

"Well, maybe he lives around there. Didn't you say he took the same bus you did yesterday?

83

But it looked almost as if he was sort of hiding by the Vernons' house. I wonder if—"

She broke off as T. J. frowned and shook his head slightly. Clearly he didn't want her to mention the missing guitar around Tracy. Julie rode in silence until her sister braked to a stop at Market Street.

"Thanks, Trace!" Julie said, stepping out of the car. "Tell Mom I'll be home soon."

"Yeah, thanks," echoed T. J.

As Tracy drove off, Julie fished the scrap of paper Mrs. Buzbee had given her out of her jacket pocket. They walked down the sidewalk, scanning the addresses. It didn't take long to find number six, a narrow Victorian house with pots of ivy on the front stoop. "I hope she's home," Julie said, ringing the bell.

The door was opened immediately by a tall black woman flanked by two small children. The girl's hair was in a dozen little braids capped with colored beads. The boy wore his hair in a soft buzz of curls. The woman was carrying a folding stroller hooked over one arm.

"Yes?" she asked when she saw Julie and T. J. on the steps.

"Um, hello," said Julie. "Are you Tullie, Louisa Knight's sister?"

"Yes, I am," said the woman. "And who are you?"

"Well, we know the Vernons, the family she works for," said T. J. "And I just needed to ask her something."

"We didn't have her phone number," Julie added. "But the neighbor had *your* address."

"You mean Mrs. Buzbee, no doubt," Tullie said with a chuckle. "I'm surprised she doesn't have Louisa's phone number—and my own, too. Not to mention our birthdates!"

"I know," said Julie, with an understanding smile.

"We get pizza!" crowed the little girl suddenly. She looked to be about three years old.

The woman laughed and took the child by the hand. "Come down the steps carefully," she said. "Hold the handrail." She turned to Julie and T. J. "We were just on our way out to dinner.

Why do you want my sister? And why not just go right to the house if you don't have her phone number? Why look for her here?"

"Well, because I'm filling in for her, cat-sitting for the Vernons," T. J. explained. "And I have . . . some questions."

"We just needed to talk to her," Julie added. "But she's away for several days, you know."

"She's away? Since when?" Tullie asked. She unfolded the stroller, and the little girl climbed in. Tullie fastened the seatbelt. "As far as I know she's at work as usual. Are you sure she's not around? Maybe she was busy with classes—you know, she takes evening classes some nights at the university."

"No, she's definitely gone," said T. J. "That's why the Vernons hired me to feed the cat." He explained that Ms. Knight had left the Vernons' house last Sunday, during the auction, because of a family emergency.

Tullie looked alarmed. "Emergency?"

"Your mother," Julie reminded her gently. "In the hospital?"

Tullie's eyes opened wide in surprise. "Our mother is not in the hospital, I assure you."

Julie and T. J. looked at each other. "Really?" asked Julie. "But your sister got a phone call saying she was really sick. She even said the call was from her sister," Julie added, feeling confused. Did Ms. Knight have more than one sister?

Tullie shrugged. "Well, when I last spoke to Louisa, she said she'd see us for dinner next weekend as usual. She almost always eats with us on Saturday nights."

"When did you talk to her?" T. J. asked, frowning.

"Just last night," Tullie replied. "She called to say she'll bring Chinese takeout. It's what we usually have."

"It's our favorite," the little boy spoke up. "Egg rolls! Yummy!"

"Pizza!" crowed the little girl, bouncing up and down in the stroller.

"Louisa said she's definitely coming on Saturday and she might have some exciting news to tell us," said Tullie. "So, I'm sorry—it looks as if there's been some misunderstanding. Probably Louisa just had to be away for some night class or something and couldn't feed the cat for a day or two." She took her little boy's hand and started pushing the stroller. "I'd better get that pizza ordered. My husband will be home soon."

"But wait!" Julie took a few steps after the woman. "Are you *sure* your mother isn't in the hospital? Maybe she is, but your sister just didn't want to worry you."

Tullie sighed. "I'm positive," she said, resting her hand on her son's head. "Our mother died ten years ago."

"Why would Ms. Knight tell Mrs. Vernon she needed to go away for a few days to look after her desperately ill mother, when there *is* no mother?" Julie asked as they walked back down the street.

"Maybe because she stole the silver guitar

and wants to sell it!" T. J. fumed. "That's probably where she is right now—wheeling and dealing and selling that guitar."

"Well, we'd better tell the Vernons what's happened. If nothing else, they need to know that their housekeeper lied to them," Julie said. She stopped at the corner as a city bus pulled up at the curb. The door opened, and passengers filed off the bus onto the sidewalk.

"They're coming home the day after tomorrow," T. J. said morosely. "We'll tell them when they get home—if we haven't found the real guitar by then."

The bus pulled away, and Julie and T. J. started crossing the street. Then Julie clutched T. J.'s arm. "There's that boy again!" she hissed.

A boy in a black baseball cap had jumped off the bus and was standing in the shadow of a storefront awning. His hat shaded his eyes and his head was turned toward the shop window, but Julie was certain it was Matt, the boy from the guitar shop.

Was he *following* them?

She and T. J. crossed the street, and Matt joined the other pedestrians. He walked behind the crowd, carrying his skateboard, up the next block. Whenever Julie looked over her shoulder, he seemed to turn away and gaze at store windows or flyers tacked to telephone poles.

"He's following us," Julie whispered.

"Really? I don't think so." T. J. turned abruptly and crossed the street. Julie ran to catch up with him as he strode over to Matt, who was looking into the window of a hardware store. "Hey, Matt," he said.

The boy raised his eyes. "Oh, hi!" He set his skateboard on the sidewalk and steadied it with one foot. "Where's your board? Want me to show you how to do a kick flip?"

"Definitely!" said T. J. "Some other time, though. I've got to get home now."

"Okay," Matt said. "Catch you later!" He waved at Julie and pushed off on his skateboard.

"See? He's not following us." T. J. said to Julie.

Julie watched Matt jump expertly off the curb on his skateboard. "But remember, he was at the music shop that day. What if *he* stole the real guitar, and now he's following us to make sure we don't go to the police about the fake one? Maybe he's trying to keep an eye on us."

T. J. looked surprised. "How could he be the thief? He's just hanging out, skating and stuff. I think you're getting paranoid."

As they walked on toward the corner where they would part company, Julie was deep in thought. Images from the afternoon played in her mind: Jasper lying on the couch, with someone hidden out of sight behind the curtain; Mrs. Buzbee peering through the Vernons' living room window; Ms. Knight's sister, Tullie, telling them their mother had died ten years ago ... And now this boy. Was Matt just riding around the city, practicing his skateboard tricks? Or could he have something to do with Danny Kendricks's stolen guitar? She felt on edge suddenly, as if danger lurked but she couldn't quite see where.

"T. J.," she said as a trolley car clattered past, "we have to be careful."

"Of what?"

"I'm not sure. But we think there's been a crime, right? And we're the ones who discovered it."

"Yeah, but why do we need to be careful? We're not the ones who stole the guitar!"

"Well, we didn't steal the real guitar," Julie corrected him. "But somebody did, and the thief might guess we're on to him." Whoever had stolen the guitar was going to be nervous—and nervous people could be dangerous.

T. J. shrugged. "We're *not* really on to him— or her. I mean, we don't really know who stole it. That's the whole problem." He sighed. "Anyway, can you come with me again after school tomorrow? Mrs. Buzbee has her eye on everything, so maybe she'll have seen something . . . something that will give us a clue to who stole the guitar. At least it should be easy to get her talking."

"Yeah, but she's still a suspect, too," Julie reminded him.

"Well, then if she says something that proves she's the thief, we'll be in luck!"

They said good-bye, and Julie headed home. She found herself looking over her shoulder as she walked. Was that Matt again, ducking into the shadow of the buildings? Julie started running. She ran all the way home, listening for footsteps pursuing her. When she arrived at her building, she stopped, panting, and looked all around.

There was no sign of Matt. Had she shaken him off, or had he not been there at all? Was she simply getting paranoid, as T. J. had said?

Even if Matt was harmless, she and T. J. would have to be extra careful. A thief who felt desperate might do anything to stop them, Julie knew. It might be only a matter of time before the thief realized they were on his—or her—trail.

9
FOOTSTEPS IN AN EMPTY ROOM

Julie found it comforting to be home again, helping Mom and Tracy make dinner. They listened to the radio while they prepared the meal, dancing around each other as they reached for the frying pan or a wooden spoon. Julie laughed as Tracy twirled her around. Then the music ended and the news came on. Tracy reached over to change the station, but Julie said, "No, wait!" The newscaster was talking about the number of dead seagulls, herons, pelicans, and other seabirds that had washed up on both sides of the bay since the oil spill.

"Thousands were injured," said the newscaster solemnly. "Only a small fraction have been rescued alive. The tanker's captain, Harold Beauthorpe, claims that fog and rough seas contributed to the wreck. He is recovering in the hospital after a—"

"That stupid ship's captain," Julie broke in, fuming. "This is all his fault."

"I don't think it's been determined yet exactly how the spill happened," said Mom.

"He's a bird killer." Julie pressed her lips together tightly. She reached for a potato and peeled it with sharp, angry movements.

"I'm sure he feels bad about the oil spill," Mom continued. "It was an accident."

"Well, he must not have been paying attention to where he was steering the boat—and now millions of gallons of oil are polluting our bay and killing the birds. He should be put in prison for the rest of his life for being so careless." Julie's voice trembled.

Mom raised her eyebrows. "You're jumping to conclusions, honey. It's easy to do that when you don't know all the facts."

"Well, Mrs. Duncan showed us a film about oil spills. The poor birds were dripping with black oil. It soaks into their feathers and the birds can't fly or eat—"

Tracy reached over and gave Julie's ponytail a reassuring tug. "But the auction is going to raise a lot of money and get them all cleaned up."

Julie refused to be comforted so easily. "Of course I hope we raise a ton of money—but I think that ships with oil shouldn't even be allowed out in the ocean at all. The spill is totally the oil company's fault!"

Mom smiled ruefully. "You have to consider why the ship was full of oil in the first place."

"Why?" Julie couldn't see any reason why a tanker ship full of dirty black oil should be sailing in the sparkling waters of the San Francisco Bay, where birds dived down for fish and built nests along the shore.

"Well," replied Mom gently, "it's because in our society we use oil—to heat our homes, to make our cars run—for all sorts of things. If we built different kinds of machines that weren't dependent on oil for fuel, then we wouldn't need big ships full of oil to deliver it for our use."

Julie hadn't thought of it that way before.

"Hey," said Tracy. She leaned across the counter and turned up the radio. "The reporter just said something about how the captain had blacked out. They think he might have had a heart attack."

"I'd heard that he collapsed shortly before the ship scraped the rocks near the lighthouse," Mom said, nodding. "But I hadn't heard why. Poor fellow. I hope he recovers."

Julie remained silent. She hadn't known about the captain's possible heart attack.

"Is he going to die?" she asked after a moment. Rock music was playing on the radio now—a wailing guitar.

"He almost did," Tracy reported. "But he was revived and is recovering now in the hospital."

"But where was the copilot?" Julie pressed. Her dad was a pilot and never flew a commercial airplane without another pilot in the cockpit. That way if anything went wrong, help was at hand. One time, she remembered, many years ago, her dad had become sick with a stomach flu in the middle of a long transatlantic flight. His copilot was able to take over and fly the plane for the remainder of the trip, and her dad could lie down and rest. "Wasn't there someone else who could have taken over?"

"I believe the accident happened too fast. But that's a good question," Mom said as she put the casserole in the oven.

"Or they should have built the ship to be stronger," suggested Julie. "So a rock couldn't so easily rip into it."

"Another good point," said Mom. "But making oil tankers stronger will cost money, and that will increase the price of oil and gasoline to consumers—people like us."

"Yeah," added Tracy. "We were just talking about that at school in my social studies class. How Americans are always complaining about the price of oil in this country, even though it's much more expensive in other countries, and we use more than people in other countries use."

Julie sighed. It was all more complicated than she'd thought—not quite so clear-cut who the bad guys were.

"Speaking of raising money for the birds," Mom said, "I've got to finish the new beaded handbags I'm donating to the auction. I'd like you girls to come straight home tomorrow after school and help me in the shop."

"Oh—sorry, Mom," Tracy said. "I've signed up to be a math tutor at the library for an hour after school, remember?"

Mom nodded. "I do remember. Well, afterward then. How about it, Julie?"

Julie hesitated, but she knew T. J. could feed the cat and talk to Mrs. Buzbee without her. "Okay," she said with an inward sigh. "I'll come straight home."

After dinner she phoned T. J. to tell him.

"Rats," he said. "*Promise* you'll come the day after that! That's when the Vernons are getting home, and I'm going to have to tell them about the guitar." He groaned. "It'll be easier if you're there with me."

"I promise," Julie told him.

THE SILVER GUITAR

The next day at school, Mrs. Wagner, the art teacher, set out fabric paints and brushes on a table at the front of the classroom. She passed around needles and colored embroidery floss. Julie decided to outline her sketch of the pelican with tiny French knots. She threaded her needle with blue floss.

"I wish you were coming with me after school," T. J. muttered as he passed her desk on his way to the table of paint. "I had nightmares all night about thieves stealing everything out of the Vernons' house. The beds and couches and even Mister Precious. Everything! And then the police came and arrested *me*." He selected some silver paint and returned to his seat, shoulders hunched.

Julie craned her neck to look at T. J.'s quilt square. He had painted a dolphin holding a guitar in its flippers. T. J. looked up and met her gaze. His expression was anxious. Then he dipped his brush into the fabric paint and started applying silver to the little guitar.

Julie began working carefully on her pelican.

She tried to make the delicate knots as neatly as Mrs. Wagner had demonstrated, but her blue thread kept tangling, and then she pricked her thumb with the needle. "Ow!" she cried.

"Take it slowly, Julie, and you'll get it right," said the teacher comfortingly as she walked past Julie's desk.

Julie resumed stitching, but her thoughts were as tangled as the blue thread. *Poor T. J.,* Julie thought. His anxiety hovered like a gray fog. His nightmares were just symbols of all his worries, she knew. But that didn't make the idea of thieves taking everything out of the Vernons' house less horrible—

A vision of the curtains stirring in the library flashed into her mind, and Julie sucked in her breath. "T. J.," she whispered across the aisle, "what if this isn't just about the guitar? I mean, what if the thief has stolen *other* things from the Vernons—and replaced *them*, too?"

He stared at her with wide eyes. "It would be a nightmare," he whispered back. "My nightmare come true. And I would be the prime suspect."

Julie hurried home after school, glancing over her shoulder at every corner, on the lookout for Matt and his skateboard, but she saw no sign of him. The bell jangled when she opened the door of Gladrags. The shop was quiet, as it always was in the lull before the after-school crowd came in.

"Hi, honey," Mom greeted her. "I left a snack on the kitchen table for you—go on up and eat it first. Then I need price tags on this new shipment of candles."

"Okay," Julie said. She looked with interest at the scented candles Mom was unpacking from a large cardboard box. The candles were all shaped like musical instruments: violins, trumpets, pianos, and guitars. Julie sighed. Was there no getting away from reminders of the stolen guitar?

"Thanks, Mom!" Julie said, and headed up to their apartment. Mom had left a cheese and onion sandwich on a plate, along with some cookies and a sliced apple. After pouring herself a tall glass of apple juice, Julie sat down with her drink and took a bite of the sandwich.

It was very peaceful in the kitchen, but Julie felt on edge. T. J. was heading to the Vernons' house right now. Would Jasper be there? Would Mrs. Buzbee say anything that would help them figure out who had stolen the silver guitar? She imagined T. J. in the library with the guitars and other treasures. Were there other fakes among Mr. Vernon's collections? How could they possibly know?

Suddenly Julie stopped chewing. Had she heard something? Yes—there it was again: footsteps, just above her.

She set down her half-eaten sandwich and stood up. Could T. J. be upstairs? But he was going straight to the Vernons' house after school. Who could be up there in the empty apartment?

Was it someone looking for the guitar?

The thief couldn't possibly know that it was hidden in the back of her closet, right?

She slipped off her shoes and, leaving her apartment, quietly walked up the stairs to the next floor. She stood outside the Ogilvies' apartment, ears alert for any sound.

Sure enough, she heard someone moving around. She heard light tapping, as if someone was hammering. Someone was definitely inside.

Taking a deep breath, Julie knocked. "Hello? Who's there?" she called. But no one answered.

She had a sudden thought: Could Matt have followed her home? He had been there that day in the music shop—and did he hear them say the guitar had belonged to Danny Kendricks? Could Matt somehow know that T. J. had hidden the guitar in the upstairs apartment? Was he poking around the apartment now, trying to find where T. J. had stashed it?

Julie told herself there was no need to be afraid of Matt, but she hurried back down the stairs and into her apartment. She closed the door with a feeling of relief, then went to her bedroom closet and peeked inside. Yes, the broken guitar was still stashed in the back of her closet. She looked out her window. A thick fog was settling over the city, shrouding the buildings across the street in mist.

Julie finished her sandwich and went down to the shop. Mom sat on a stool behind the sales counter, chatting with a customer.

"I'll take the green one and the blue one, darling," the customer said, setting two large, colorful tote bags on the glass counter.

Mom started wrapping the purchases. She looked up as Julie approached. "Julie, you remember Mrs. Ogilvie?"

Julie nodded. "Hello," she said politely. "Is your new apartment near here?"

"Close enough to get back to Gladrags when there's something special I need, I'm glad to say." Mrs. Ogilvie packed her new things into a large plastic shopping bag. "We were happy here, but the rooms were small, and all those stairs were too much. Time to move on!" She paid for her purchases and turned to leave.

Julie saw Mr. Ogilvie, a stout man with a cane, waiting for his wife just inside the door to the shop. A taxi idled at the curb.

"Hello, Mr. Ogilvie," Mom called to him.

He smiled and nodded, and then eyed his wife's shopping bag. "We don't have room for more new things, dear," he said.

"Just a couple of tote bags, Harry," Mrs. Ogilvie replied. "They'll come in handy for travel."

"They're very pretty," Mr. Ogilvie said. He turned to Mrs. Albright. "Nice to see you again."

"Thanks for stopping in," Mom said. "Good luck in your new home, and come again!"

Julie sat at the counter and stuck price tags on all the candles while Mom served the after-school crowd. Soon Tracy arrived and helped Julie price a shipment of macramé plant hangers. Then Mom locked up Gladrags for the night, and they went upstairs for dinner.

As Julie climbed the back stairs behind Mom and Tracy, it occurred to her that it might have been Mr. Ogilvie up in the empty apartment while his wife shopped at Gladrags, and not Matt—or a thief. The Ogilvies' lease lasted till the end of the month, after all. Perhaps they had come back just to check on the apartment or even just to say good-bye. Julie remembered the way she had stood in her bedroom at her old house on moving day almost two years ago, just soaking up the feel of the place before she left. Soaking in the *vibes*.

Good thing the broken guitar was in *her* closet now, Julie reflected. What a surprise the Ogilvies would have had if they'd found it in their empty apartment when they went up to say good-bye!

10
TRAPPED!

The next day at school, Julie and T. J. sat together while they added the finishing touches to their quilt squares.

T. J. spoke in hushed tones as he stitched lines of silver thread for his dolphin's guitar strings. "When I got to the Vernons' last night to feed Mister Precious, guess what—I caught Mrs. Buzbee peeking in the windows again."

"What did you do?" Julie asked.

"I stepped up behind her very quietly and then asked if I could help her with anything. I must have scared her, because she jumped!"

Julie had to laugh. "Serves her right." She smoothed out the embroidery floss so that it would not tangle.

"Mrs. Buzbee said she was checking on

things." T. J. wrinkled his nose. "Maybe she was just being nosy as usual, but maybe she was really planning another theft."

"Does she know that the Vernons are coming back today?"

"I have no idea. We didn't really chat." T. J. paused and then added, "Mr. Vernon phoned from Seattle and asked me to come over after school today so that they can pay me for looking after Mister Precious . . ." His voice trailed off. "That's when I have to tell them about the guitar."

"I'm coming with you, don't worry," Julie assured him.

T. J. gave her a grateful look. "I have to go to a Boy Scout meeting first, so let's meet outside Grace Cathedral at four o'clock. Then we'll walk to the Vernons' together." He sighed. "I'm not looking forward to this. They're going to think the missing guitar is all my fault."

"Not necessarily," said Julie. "We'll just tell them the truth of what we know—that's all we can do."

"But what if they don't believe us? They might think you're my accomplice." The bell rang, signaling the end of class. T. J. sighed again and turned to go.

"See you soon," he said, and headed into the hallway, shoulders slumping.

After school, Julie told her mother she was taking the bus over to Nob Hill to help T. J. at the Vernons' again, which was the truth. Julie checked her watch as the bus pulled up outside Grace Cathedral. She was five minutes late to meet T. J., but he wasn't in front of the cathedral gates yet. Maybe the Boy Scout meeting was lasting longer than he'd expected.

A spring mist drifted down from the great cathedral's spire. Julie zipped up her sweatshirt and waited. Ten minutes passed, and then fifteen. Had T. J. forgotten they were to meet and gone on to the Vernons' house, thinking he'd find her there instead?

At last she saw a boy coming toward her through the fog. "About time!" she called—then she gasped when she realized it was not T. J. at all, but Matt.

"Hi, Julie," he said. He leaned casually against the gates of the cathedral. "I have a surprise for you."

"What kind of surprise?" she asked, wondering how Matt knew her name. T. J. must have mentioned it when he was hanging around with Matt learning skateboard tricks.

Matt smiled. "The kind you're going to like!"

"Well, what is it?" Distracted, she looked past him, up the street. Where *was* T. J.?

"I'll give you one clue!" His voice was teasing. "It's silver."

She snapped her head around. "What are you talking about?"

He laughed. "Let's just say it's something you've been hoping for."

Julie's heart pounded. He could only mean one thing. "The guitar?" she asked breathlessly.

Matt shrugged, his eyes sparkling with mischief.

"But how do *you* know about it?" asked Julie.

"Did T. J. tell you?" She was surprised, but she knew the boys had been hanging out. Maybe T. J. had told him everything.

"Let's just say I have my sources!" Matt grinned at her.

"This is great news," Julie told him, limp with relief. "As soon as T. J. gets here—"

"Oh, he's already waiting for you."

"What?" Confused, Julie stared at him.

"Yep." Matt nodded. "He's at my house. Come on. The surprise is for both of you." He jumped on his skateboard and started skimming along the sidewalk. "It's not far. Just a block."

"Wait up!" She hurried after him, running to keep up and pelting him with questions. "So where *is* the guitar?" she asked. "Where did you find it? Is it okay—I mean, no damage?"

Matt stopped outside a high wall with a painted red gate, flipping his skateboard high into the air with his foot and catching it neatly. "T. J.'s in my clubhouse," he said. "Come on!"

"Hold on a minute," said Julie, as Matt unlatched the gate and stepped inside. "You

haven't answered a single question!" Through
the gate, she glimpsed a lush green garden and
a little blue shed surrounded by blooming rose
bushes.

"Of course not—it's a surprise!" Matt smiled
at her. "All I know is, you and your brother are
going to love it."

Julie stopped cold. "My ... *brother*?" A shiver
ran across her shoulder blades.

"If I say anything more, I'll spoil it," Matt
said cheerfully. "I hope I haven't said too much
already."

"If you don't tell me what's going on, I'm not
coming one step farther," Julie declared.

He whirled around. "But T. J. is waiting for
you!"

Julie was bewildered. This was how Alice must
have felt when she followed the white rabbit
down the hole into Wonderland. Nothing was
making sense. Suddenly a possibility occurred to
her. "Did—did the *Vernons* tell you there was a
surprise?" Was it possible that the Vernons had
known about the fake guitar the whole time after all?

Matt was walking along the gravel path leading from the gate to the blue shed, but he stopped and looked back at her. "I don't know any Vernons," he said. "Come on!"

Julie shivered again and did not follow. "Was it you, then?" she asked. "Did *you* take the real guitar?"

Matt looked blank. "I don't know what you're talking about." He turned and continued toward the blue shed.

She couldn't let him just walk away. If he hadn't stolen the guitar himself, he certainly knew *something*. She started after him, her heart pounding. Maybe he'd hidden the guitar in the shed. The wooden structure had a corrugated metal roof and was half covered in vines.

The shed door opened, and T. J. stood in the doorway. "Finally!" he shouted. "I've been waiting for ages!"

Julie walked cautiously up to him. "T. J., what's going on?"

"You tell me! I've been waiting for you."

"But we're late to the Vernons! Why did

you want to meet *here*, of all places?"

"Matt told me *you* wanted to meet here. He said you had a surprise for me, something *silver*! I was hoping . . ." His voice trailed off. "I was hoping you'd found the guitar, somehow."

They both looked at Matt.

He tilted back his black baseball cap. "You'll see! It's all part of the surprise. We're all supposed to wait right here."

"You called T. J. my *brother*," Julie said tightly. "But I don't have a brother. Who told you he was my brother?"

Now Matt looked confused. "You mean he's not? That's weird."

"Okay—what's going on, Matt?" asked T. J. "Who said we're supposed to wait here? What do you know about the stolen guitar?"

"*Stolen* guitar?" Matt pulled off his cap and twisted it. "What are *you* talking about?"

Julie pushed past the boys and peered into the shed. A tool bench ran along one wall and a pegboard hung with garden rakes and hoes ran along another. Bicycles, three of them, crowded one corner with a lawn mower. There were stacks of flowerpots, large bags of potting soil, and a metal watering can.

But there was no silver guitar.

T. J. stepped in behind Julie. "Something's really weird," he said quietly. "Matt told me that you wanted to meet here, and that we'd get a surprise. Something silver. I thought that meant you'd somehow found the stolen Strat and were bringing it here."

"I thought the exact same thing about you!" Julie whispered back frantically. "Something's really fishy."

"Oh, man." T. J.'s shoulders sagged. "We'd better get to the Vernons', then. We're late enough already!"

Julie turned to glower at Matt, who was standing in the open doorway of the shed. "That's it," she said abruptly. "We're leaving."

Matt blocked the door. "You can't leave yet!"

"Get out of our way!" snapped T. J.

Matt looked at his watch. "You have to wait—your grandparents will be here soon."

"Our *grandparents*?" Julie felt dizzy with confusion. Her grandparents lived several hours away, in Santa Rosa. What could *they* possibly know about the silver guitar?

"*My* grandparents live in Connecticut!" T. J. shouted. "And Julie isn't my sister! Matt, what happened to Danny Kendricks's silver guitar?"

"Huh? I don't know anything about that. All I know is, you're ruining the surprise," Matt said peevishly. "They told me you'd be *so* surprised, and you'd love it. But now you're spoiling everything." Quick as a shot, he was suddenly on the other side of the shed door, holding it closed. Julie heard a rasp of metal as the bolt slid into place.

"Hey!" T. J. raised his fists and pounded on the door.

"Please, don't!" Matt implored from the other side of the door. "Just wait till five o'clock, that's what they said!"

T. J. hammered harder, but Julie stood silently, her eyes scanning the shed for a way out.

Matt was holding them here—why? Because

he had been told something. By whom? Who were these so-called grandparents?

Not Julie's grandparents, and not T. J.'s. That meant Matt had been told a story by someone who wanted him to follow T. J. and Julie—and detain them.

That meant Matt was being *used*. Matt was nothing but a dupe.

Julie shuddered. She looked up at the small window above the tool bench and calculated swiftly that they could not fit through it. But on the back wall, behind the flowerpots and the bikes and the lawn mower, she could see a small door set low in the wall.

T. J. was still pounding on the door. "Look," Matt shouted, "I'll—I'll go in the house and bring us out some ice cream, if you'll just wait. Just wait fifteen minutes and they'll be here!" His voice rose pleadingly. "Just till five o'clock, that's all—and then you'll get your surprise. And—and I'll get my fifty bucks!"

11
HIDE AND SEEK

T. J. raised his fists to pound again, but Julie stopped him, her finger to her lips. "So tell us, Matt," she said sweetly into the sudden silence. "How come these grandparents of ours are going to give you so much money?"

Matt seemed grateful to talk to them. And as he began speaking, Julie pointed silently to the little door. It was a dog door built into the wall, closed with a flap. T. J. gave her a thumbs-up, and quietly they set to work moving the bikes away from the wall while Matt spoke. "I was just hanging out at the music shop a few days ago. It's pretty far from my house, but it's the best one in the city, so I go there a lot. Gary, the clerk, lets me help out sometimes and practice on the guitars. Anyway, this older man came in and asked if I'd seen two kids carrying a guitar wrapped in a blanket."

"When was this?" Julie called through the locked shed door. She wanted to keep him talking so that he wouldn't hear T. J. moving the lawn mower.

"It was the same day you two were in there, I guess." Matt's voice carried clearly to the back of the shed. "I told him I had. Then Gary told him the guitar was broken. He said you'd thought it was a Kendricks original, but it really wasn't."

Just a few big flowerpots to shift and they'd reach the dog door. Julie and T. J. lifted them together. "Go on," yelled T. J. "What did my, uh, grandfather say next?"

"Well, we went out of the shop, and I met your grandmother. She told me that they were your grandparents and wanted to surprise you with a newer, better guitar than the cheap broken one you had been playing. She said that if I helped with the surprise they'd even pay me!

That was good news because I'm saving up for a guitar of my own." His voice pleaded through the shed door. "You know how hard it is, right, T. J.? Coming up with all the dough?"

"Go on," said T. J. brusquely.

Matt continued, as if eager to explain. "They said my job was to follow you—to be sure you didn't buy another guitar yourself, maybe." He hesitated. "Well, I'm not sure. But I was supposed to bring you here and wait till five o'clock for the big surprise. And," Matt added, "if you gave me any trouble about coming here to wait, I was supposed to mention the special clue: *something silver.*"

Julie caught T. J.'s eye and knew he was thinking the same thing she was: *who are these phony grandparents?* If they could figure that out, maybe somehow everything would fall into place.

"Matt," she called, "what did the grandfather look like?"

"I don't know—just a nice old man with a cane. He seemed so pleased about the surprise. He said to do whatever it takes to keep you here with me until five o'clock, and it's almost five now!"

Julie was on her knees by the dog door. It was strung with cobwebs. Clearly no dog had used it for a long time. Julie swept the cobwebs away with her hands and wiped them on her jeans. Although she often wished she were as tall as Tracy, right now Julie was glad to be small. She led the way, silently squeezing through the dog door. The rubber flap closed behind her.

As she stood up outside the shed, something fell out of her jacket pocket. She glanced at it—it was the auction catalogue that Mrs. Vernon had given her last weekend. Julie was about to stuff it back in her pocket when a line on the back cover caught her eye: *Auction photographs courtesy of Harold and Patricia Ogilvie.*

"Come on, Julie. Help me out!" T. J. hissed. He didn't fit as easily through the dog door. Julie grabbed his hand and tugged him onto the grass. Matt was sitting on the ground, leaning against the blue door, still talking to them through the crack. "When you get your new guitar and I get mine, we should jam together," he was saying to the closed door as Julie and T. J. darted past him.

Without looking back, they flew through the gate and started running.

"Hey! Come back!" they heard Matt yell. Julie looked over her shoulder to see him leaping onto his skateboard and zooming down the sidewalk after them. Julie and T. J. careened down the next block and across the street to the Vernons' mansion.

"Hold on there!" called Mrs. Buzbee, crossing the driveway to them. "I looked out my window and saw you tearing along the street. What are you kids up to?" As Matt arrived, leaping off his skateboard, kicking it into the air and catching it, Mrs. Buzbee added in a tone of outrage, *"What's going on here?"*

Julie opened her mouth, and then shut it. What *was* going on? Could Mrs. Buzbee be the imposter grandmother? But who could the grandfather be?

Julie and T. J. turned and pounded up the front steps, followed closely by Matt, and T. J. rang the doorbell.

The front door opened, and Jasper stood there, looking surprised and a little amused. "Well, well, look what the cat dragged in," he said laconically.

"Jasper, I need to talk to you!" Mr. Vernon's voice boomed down the hall. With a groan, Jasper turned and disappeared into the house as Mrs. Vernon hurried to the door.

"Come in, kids." Mrs. Vernon ushered them into the front hall. "We've been worried, wondering where you were. Did something happen?"

"That's just what I want to know," said Mrs. Buzbee, who followed right behind Julie and T. J. as if she, too, had been included in the invitation. Matt hovered on the doorstep.

"Are you with Julie and T. J.?" Mrs. Vernon asked. Matt nodded. "Well, come along, then."

"You need to call the police," gasped Julie.

Mrs. Vernon looked alarmed. "Let's sit in the

drawing room, and you can tell us what's going on." She led them into the elegant room. "Yes, all right, you too, Mrs. Buzbee," she said as the neighbor pushed past her and sat in Mr. Vernon's deep leather chair by the fireplace.

Julie and T. J. sat side by side on a plush love-seat, still breathing hard from their run. Matt stood by the door, shifting uneasily from one leg to the other, his arms wrapped around his skateboard.

Mrs. Buzbee looked around at everyone else, bright-eyed and expectant. "This is like one of those murder mysteries set in an old mansion," she said gleefully. "Is one of us a murderer, then?"

"Not a murderer," T. J. blurted out, "but a thief!"

"Hold on, T. J." Julie nudged him in the ribs. Then she took a deep breath and turned to Mrs. Vernon. "T. J. has something to tell you. Something that happened while you were gone—"

Before she could continue, there was another shout from down the hall. A door slammed, and then Jasper yelled, "I had nothing to do with it!" Julie saw Jasper walk rapidly past the open door of the drawing room, his footsteps muffled on the thick carpet that ran down the hall. A second later Mr. Vernon strode into view, hurrying to catch up with his nephew.

"Oh, no, you don't," he said. "You're not leaving this house until you give me a full accounting of what happened," he said tersely to the young man.

"I'm telling you, I don't know anything about it!" Jasper sounded upset. "I have no idea where that guitar is, but I haven't touched it!"

Julie twisted the auction catalogue nervously in her lap. She turned to Mrs. Vernon, trying to keep her voice steady. "That's what we want to tell you about," she said quickly. "We think there's been a theft!"

Mrs. Vernon looked alarmed. "Dear, I think you'd better come in here and listen to this," she called to her husband. "Jasper, you too, please."

Mr. Vernon came into the drawing room, red-faced and upset, followed by Jasper, who looked sullen and resentful—almost as if he were sulking, thought Julie. Had Mr. Vernon just accused him of stealing the guitar?

"All right, Julie, you were saying that you and T. J. have something to tell us," Mrs. Vernon prompted.

Julie exchanged a glance with T. J. This was it, the moment he had been dreading. She gave him an encouraging nod, and he cleared his throat nervously.

"Um . . . yeah," he began. His voice trembled as he explained how he had taken the guitar off the wall to look at it more closely, and how the cat had jumped on him, and how he'd dropped the guitar. Leaving out the part about hiding it in the empty apartment, T. J. told everyone how he and Julie had taken the broken guitar to the music store to try to get it fixed and had learned that it was not Danny Kendricks's Fender Stratocaster, but a cheap fake.

"So it wasn't Jasper who took it," Mr. Vernon said. "It was *you!*"

"No—I didn't steal the *real* guitar," T. J.

protested earnestly. "But, well, we think somebody else did." T. J. squirmed. "We thought maybe the housekeeper, or someone here"— his gaze traveled from Jasper, to Mr. Vernon, to Mrs. Buzbee, and back to Mrs. Vernon—"might have, well, taken it for some reason."

"You thought *I* took the guitar?" Mrs. Buzbee shrilled, looking indignant.

"Or that you might *know* who took it," Julie said diplomatically. With a prickle of unease, she smoothed the auction catalogue in her lap and read the words on the back cover again. Flashes of memory stabbed her: footsteps on the stairs, a man with a cane, people waving to her in the street, thumps overhead in the empty apartment . . . Julie sucked in her breath. Suddenly she knew who had told Matt they were her grandparents, who had set him up to be an accessory to their crime. With a shiver, she now knew whom she and T. J. should have been seeking all along—and who had been watching them.

"We were wrong about all our suspects, T. J. I think I know who did it," Julie announced.

12
COMING CLEAN

"Harold and Patricia Ogilvie?" T. J. squinted at the catalogue Julie held out.

"Our *photographers*?" exclaimed Mrs. Vernon.

Julie turned to her. "The Ogilvies came to this house and photographed all the objects that were going to be auctioned, right?"

"That's right," said Mr. Vernon. His florid color was fading, and he no longer looked ready to boil over. "They came several times, in fact. They showed great interest in all my collections," he added proudly.

"I think maybe they weren't just taking pictures for the auction catalogue. I think maybe they were also stealing valuable things and leaving fake copies behind," Julie said in a rush of words.

Mr. Vernon looked skeptical. "That's a pretty far-fetched idea." He regarded T. J. suspiciously. "Are you sure that's all you have to tell us, young man?"

His wife put a hand on his arm. "Maybe it's time to call the police, dear."

Julie looked around the elegant room. Jasper slouched on the sofa—he looked so familiar in that posture—when had she seen him like that before? Suddenly she saw again in her mind's eye how the curtains had billowed out, sending a shaft of sunlight through the dancing dust-motes . . . and onto the glass dome with the black silk top hat . . . President Lincoln's top hat, which had looked so faded, almost rusty with age, the first time she had seen it—but that day with Jasper it had looked velvety black.

With a sharp intake of breath, Julie sat up very straight. "Mr. Vernon," she asked, "would you mind if we took a look at Abraham Lincoln's top hat?"

He frowned. "Might I ask why?"

"Well, once when I came here with T. J. to help

feed Mister Precious, we were in the library, and
I noticed that the hat didn't look so old and faded
anymore. I—I didn't think anything of it at the
time." She'd been too distracted, frightened by
the knowledge that someone was hiding behind
the curtain, but she didn't mention that now. Julie
glanced at Jasper. He quirked an eyebrow at her,
seeming amused, as if he remembered that
particular day, too. "But now," Julie continued
resolutely, "I wonder whether . . ."

"—whether *it's* a fake, too?" T. J. said in a
whisper, his eyes big.

Mr. Vernon sighed and stood up. "Well, let's
just go take a look." His tone was dubious, but
he led them down the hallway to the library.
Mr. Vernon entered first and walked over to the
dome containing the black top hat. The black
satin gleamed under the glass.

"Look how clean and black the fabric is,"
Julie pointed out. "It doesn't look like something
that's over a hundred years old."

Mr. Vernon looked mildly at the hat, then
peered closer and frowned. "What in the

world?" He lifted the glass dome.

Julie held her breath. "The hatmaker's label," she whispered. "Check if it's there."

She knew it would not be.

Mr. Vernon turned the hat upside down. "It isn't!" he thundered. "This is an obvious fake. Someone has stolen Lincoln's hat!"

"I was afraid of that," said Julie. "And there might be other things missing, too."

Mr. Vernon's eyes narrowed. "And to think those photographers, those *Ogilvies*"— he said darkly, as if it were a dirty word—"to think they were probably here stealing my valuable things and leaving me with fakes, right under my nose!"

"Such a betrayal," said Mrs. Vernon. "We trusted them."

"I guess that's why they were successful," Julie said. "And if T. J. hadn't accidentally broken the guitar when the cat jumped on him, no one would ever have realized it was a fake—until the auction."

"And how embarrassing *that* would have been," Mr. Vernon said. "People might have thought we were trying to pull a scam."

Julie and T. J. exchanged a swift, guilty look. That was exactly what they had thought.

"And while the authorities were investigating *us* for selling fake antiques," added Mrs. Vernon grimly, "those shameless Ogilvies would have sold the things they'd stolen and disappeared."

"I think maybe that's what they're trying to do right now," Matt said suddenly. He had been standing apart from the others, seeming uneasy in this unfamiliar company. "I bet that's why they told me to keep you two busy and out of the way until five o'clock—to give them time to make their getaway, before you told the Vernons about the real guitar being switched for a fake."

"And who are *you*, dear?" Mrs. Vernon looked baffled.

Matt flushed. "I'm Matt Atkinson. I live down the street a few blocks from here. I met T. J. and Julie at the music store on Haight Street the day they brought the silver guitar in. That's the same day I met their grandpar—I mean the Ogilvies."

Quickly Julie told how the Ogilvies had asked Matt to help plan a surprise for her and T. J. She left out the part about how Matt had shut them into the shed and how they had escaped. "The Ogilvies told Matt they were our grandparents and were sorry our guitar was broken. They were going to get us a new one and asked him to help make it a special surprise."

"They promised me fifty bucks if I would bring T. J. and Julie to my house," Matt said sheepishly. "I was supposed to keep them waiting in the garden shed until five o'clock. That's when they said they'd bring the guitar—*and* my money." He looked down at his feet. "I was stupid to believe them," he mumbled, glancing over at T. J. and Julie. "I'm really sorry."

"You weren't the only one who was fooled by them," said Mrs. Vernon kindly.

"Hey, you wanted the dough," said T. J. more bluntly. "I know how it is when you're saving up for a guitar."

Mr. Vernon stood up. "I say it's definitely time to call the police." He left the room.

Mrs. Vernon gave Julie a hug. "Oh, your mother will be horrified to hear what's been going on. We must get you home." She turned to T. J. "Your parents will never let you cat-sit for us again!"

"You mean you would hire me again?" T. J. asked. "Even after all this?"

"Of course we would hire you. Jasper told me you were very punctual and looked after Mister Precious wonderfully." Mrs. Vernon gave her nephew a tight smile. "Jasper said you and Julie even took care of *him* when he was feeling under the weather."

Surprised, Julie looked over at Jasper. She felt her cheeks redden as he dropped her a wink.

Mr. Vernon rejoined them in the library. "The police are on their way," he announced. "They'll want to take statements from you three kids. Let's call your parents and tell them what's happening."

As they waited for the police to arrive, Jasper turned to Julie. "You told T. J. you were wrong about all your suspects. So tell us—who *did* you suspect of stealing the guitar and substituting the fake?"

Julie and T. J. glanced at each other.

"Well," Julie said after a long pause, "we sort of suspected each of you."

"Wait a minute!" Jasper looked indignant. "Why would you suspect *me*?"

Because we jumped to conclusions, Julie thought. She had suspected nearly everyone based on what she thought was evidence. *Just as the oil spill wasn't really the ship captain's fault.* Mom had helped her see that the blame for the oil spill in the bay was not clear-cut. Now Julie realized that the theft of the silver guitar was also more complex than she and T. J. had first thought.

"Go on," Mrs. Vernon urged. "I want to hear what you were thinking."

Hesitantly, Julie outlined their suspicions. "Well, all of you had access to the house, and at first everybody seemed to have a motive. For instance, we suspected Jasper because, well, he doesn't have a job and so we thought he might want the money he could get for Kendricks's guitar. And when we came over to feed the cat, there was someone hiding behind the curtains here"—Julie turned and gestured toward the tall windows—"while Jasper was watching TV."

At his aunt's exclamation of surprise, Jasper groaned. "Oh, all right, I had some friends in for a party," he admitted. "When the kids came in to feed the cat that afternoon, my new girlfriend Holly was still here, watching a movie on TV with me. She hid behind the curtain when we heard the door open." He turned to his aunt and uncle. "I was afraid you two had come home early." He shrugged. "The kids have eagle eyes."

"Well, Julie does," said T. J. generously. "She's the one who noticed someone was hiding. It kind of scared us!"

"I'm sorry to hear it," said Mrs. Vernon, giving her nephew a stern frown.

Jasper looked genuinely contrite. "Aunt Eleanor, I think you'll really like Holly—I want you to meet her. Does it help to know that she's taking a paramedic course and she's persuaded me to sign up?"

Mrs. Vernon pursed her lips, but her frown softened. "Well, that might help a bit," she said.

Mr. Vernon cleared his throat. "Go on," he said to Julie. "Who else did you suspect?"

Mrs. Buzbee chimed in. "Why, they suspected me," she said brightly. This time she looked as if she was rather pleased to be included.

For once, Julie thought to herself with a smile, *something really* is *going on—and she's part of it all.* She realized that the nosy neighbor meant no harm; she was nosy only because she was lonely.

Julie gave her a smile. "We did suspect you, but only because you're often . . . around."

Jasper snorted. Mrs. Buzbee looked gleeful.

"And did you suspect us, too?" asked Mr. Vernon, his eyebrows raised.

"Um . . . not exactly," Julie hedged, avoiding T. J.'s eyes.

"What's that sound?" Mrs. Vernon asked.

"I didn't hear anything," said Mr. Vernon.

Everyone fell silent, and Julie thought she heard the click of a door latch closing.

"There it is again—someone's come into the

house!" cried Mrs. Vernon. She leaned forward and clutched her husband's arm.

Now Julie could clearly hear footsteps coming down the hall.

Mr. Vernon leaped to his feet. "Who's there?"

The footsteps paused. "It's just me," came a soft voice, and a moment later Ms. Knight stepped into the room.

"Oh, my dear Louisa, you gave us a fright," said Mrs. Vernon, sinking back into her chair.

Ms. Knight looked around at everyone. "What's going on?" she asked.

Mrs. Buzbee's eyes danced. "Oh, lots and lots—just wait till you hear. *You* were a suspect, too!"

Ms. Knight blinked. "A suspect?" Her purse fell from her hand and she took a step back; then she reached for the door frame to steady herself. "I didn't do anything," she whispered.

Why, she looks guilty, Julie thought to herself. Was Ms. Knight somehow involved with the Ogilvies' scheme after all? As the housekeeper, she could have helped them replace the valuables with the fakes and sneak the real items out of the house without raising suspicion. The Ogilvies might have paid her for her help— and her silence.

"Yes, you did," T. J. piped up. "You lied."

Ms. Knight flashed him a stricken look.

"Now, T. J., whatever do you mean?" Mrs. Vernon sounded indignant.

"I mean people who died ten years ago aren't still in the hospital," T. J. replied.

Ms. Knight ducked her head. After a moment she lifted it and turned to Mrs. Vernon, who was staring at her in surprise. "He's right. And I owe you an apology. I shouldn't have said my mother was ill—it wasn't true. At the auction, that TV producer, Dick Weston, told me there was a small part in a new series he's making that I might be perfect for. He invited me to audition right away—a screen test! You know of my interest in film and how I want to be an actress." Ms. Knight stared down at her hands. "I figured it was a long shot, and I felt silly telling you I wanted to audition. So I made up an excuse and said my mother was ill ... and, well, I drove down to Los Angeles for a few days." She glanced at her employer, shamefaced. "I'm sorry for lying. It was wrong of me."

"Did you get the part?" asked Julie with interest. Just think what Tracy would say if Julie could tell her she knew a real television actress!

But Ms. Knight shook her head ruefully. "Not even a callback." With a sigh, she sat down in a chair next to Mrs. Buzbee.

The old lady patted Ms. Knight on the arm reassuringly. "You'll make it someday, dear," she said. "I hear you singing opera in the shower. Lovely voice. Maybe that's your ticket."

Ms. Knight raised her eyebrows.

"Sound travels through open windows, you know," said Mrs. Buzbee, smiling slyly.

Such a nosy neighbor! thought Julie with a chuckle.

A heavy knock sounded on the front door, making Julie jump. The police had arrived.

The cat, startled, leaped from the arm of the couch into Julie's lap. She winced at the dig of sharp claws on her thigh.

"Mister Precious is an animal of discerning taste," said Mr. Vernon fondly as he went to meet the police. "Julie is his hero."

"She's *our* hero," said Mrs. Vernon. "And T. J., too."

13
GOOD VIBRATIONS

On the day of the benefit auction for the seabirds, Julie and her family arrived early at the Vernons' mansion. Mom was donating three of her popular beaded handbags, and Julie and Tracy helped set up the display.

"Wouldn't it be great if Stella Ethan or another celebrity bought one?" Tracy murmured to Julie as Mom arranged the colorful handbags on a table. "Mom's bags could start a trend!"

The drawing room furniture had been pushed to the walls, and rows of folding chairs were set up in the middle, facing the fireplace. The auctioneer's microphone stood on a podium in front of the fireplace, and hanging above the mantel was the finished quilt.

Julie gazed up at it. The quilt seemed to glow

in the spring sunlight coming through the tall windows. The finished project was large enough to cover a queen-sized bed, and had been edged with blue and green fabric to suggest the sea. The squares were embroidered or painted or patched with symbols of ocean life—fish, crabs, dolphins, turtles, and soaring birds. There were also boats, sand castles, and even a lighthouse. Some were realistically drawn and others were more whimsical, like Julie's pelican with sunglasses and T. J.'s dolphin playing a guitar. Julie studied the quilt and felt a rush of satisfaction as she read the sign propped beneath it on the mantelpiece:

Handmade by the Students of
Jack London Elementary School, San Francisco

"Far out!" Tracy said admiringly, coming to Julie's side.

"Everybody did such a good job," said Julie with pride.

Other items to be auctioned were set up all

around the large room. Danny Kendricks's guitar was mounted on the wall between two long mirrors, and its silver gleam caught the eyes of the people starting to arrive.

Mr. and Mrs. Vernon walked over with Julie's mom. "We're so thankful we got the guitar back safely. And just in time for the auction, too," Mrs. Vernon was saying in a hushed voice. "Those awful Ogilvies were caught trying to board a plane to Mexico. In their luggage the police found dozens of stolen items."

"They've both been arrested for theft and attempted fraud," Mr. Vernon added.

Julie's mother shook her head. "It makes me shiver to think they were living in the apartment above us."

"It's so creepy," said Tracy. "They seemed so normal, but they were fakes—just like the fakes they left in place of the things they stole."

"Well, we knew they were artists," Julie pointed out. "We just didn't know they were *scam* artists!" Everyone chuckled.

"They were scam artists indeed, and very

clever ones," Mr. Vernon said. "The police filled us in on their scheme, and I'd say we were very lucky that T. J. broke that guitar, or they would have made off with quite a haul.

"The Ogilvies would go to people's homes to photograph valuable antiques—sometimes for auctions, sometimes for insurance purposes," he continued. "They took pictures and then used the photos to get cheap duplicates to leave in place of the valuables they took. By the time the fakes were discovered, the originals would be sold and the Ogilvies would be long gone."

"They came to the owners' houses first to photograph the originals, and then they returned on the pretext of needing to take new pictures because the light wasn't just right the first time," Mrs. Vernon added.

"That's exactly what they did at your house!" Julie exclaimed. "T. J. said that the first time he went to feed Mister Precious, the Ogilvies were there, taking more photos. That must be when they brought in the fakes and substituted them for the real things." She could recall T. J.'s voice that day up in the empty apartment: *"The only other people around were the photographers, and they were in another room on the other side of the house, taking more photos for the auction catalogue."*

"They hid their loot in an attic crawl space of their old apartment," said Mr. Vernon. "The police recovered quite a haul of stolen goods, including a number of things from our house: a Ming Dynasty vase, several rare coins, and a sketch by Van Gogh, as well as the silver guitar and Lincoln's hat."

Bumps and thumps at midnight . . . "I heard them!" Julie said. "Footsteps in the empty apartment at odd hours, and hammering. They must have been closing up the crawl space after stashing their loot." Julie realized with a shiver that when she and T. J. had been up there with the broken guitar, the *real* guitar had been somewhere nearby in the very same apartment. If only they had known!

"They had every detail planned," Mr. Vernon fumed. "The stolen items were being sold to various collectors around the country. They had already arranged sales of most of the items, and were planning to retrieve them and ship them off to their new owners, and then hide out in Mexico for a while. But thanks to you and T. J., they had to flee early, leaving their most recently stolen goods—*our* things—for the police to find."

"Low-down crooks, the pair of them," said Mrs. Vernon. "And the lowest thing they did was to rope in a child to help them!"

Julie nodded. "Matt sure feels dumb, letting himself get conned like that." She pointed to Matt, who was standing with a throng of people admiring the silver guitar. "T. J. invited him to come today, but at first he wasn't going to. He's so embarrassed."

As if he'd heard his name, Matt glanced in their direction. Julie waved to him and he started walking over, accompanied by T. J.

"I hope Matt has learned a lesson," Mrs. Vernon said thoughtfully. "But a boy who wants to earn an honest dollar to buy himself a guitar might try asking me after the auction," she added as the boys approached. "We have a lot of odd jobs that need doing."

"There might be *two* boys asking, in that case," T. J. said with a grin. He looked around the room, which was now packed with people. "I wonder who will buy the guitar?"

Mr. Vernon smiled. "It'll be fun to see how high the bidding goes."

"Maybe you should bid on it yourself," Julie suggested shyly. "I mean, that way you could still keep your guitar—"

"While donating money to a very good cause!" Mr. Vernon laughed. "I thought of that myself, and it's tempting! But I'm ready to part with it." He winked at his wife. "Clear out the house a little. Free up some space."

"Just to make room for new things, if I know you!" Mrs. Vernon teased, linking her arm through his.

The auction committee chairwoman rang her handbell, and the crowd of people in the drawing room grew silent as she began to speak. "Good afternoon, everyone! Thank you all for coming to this event. The proceeds we raise today will benefit the rehabilitation of injured seabirds, so don't be shy—bid often and bid high! Now, I hope you've all had a chance to look around the room at the items being auctioned today and made a long list of all the fabulous things you just can't live without!"

People chuckled and took their seats. Julie went to sit in the front row with Mom and Tracy and the Vernons. She saw Matt and beckoned him to an empty seat in their row.

Mrs. Vernon joined the auction chairwoman at the podium. "As you all may have noticed, we have a very special auction item today." She pointed to the colorful quilt hanging over the fireplace mantel. "I'd like to thank all the students at Jack London Elementary School, right here in San Francisco, who made the quilt squares. Thanks also to the parents and staff who helped the children get everything sewn together in time for today's auction." Mrs. Vernon held up her hand to forestall the audience's applause.

"Finally, I'd like to recognize fifth-grader Julie Albright, the student body president at Jack London Elementary, for coming up with the idea of donating the quilt to benefit the bird-rescue effort." Mrs. Vernon smiled over at Julie. "Julie, please stand up."

Julie stood, and she felt a warm flush creep up from her toes to her cheeks as everyone applauded. T. J. gave her a standing ovation.

Then the bell rang, and the bidding began.

Going ... going ... gone! Mrs. Albright's beaded handbags went to three pop singers.

"Mom's going to be the new designer for the jet set—wait and see!" crowed Tracy, squeezing Julie's arm.

The quilt fetched a high price—and the person who bought it was none other than Stella Ethan, the actress. Lights flashed as photographers snapped pictures of her holding it in her arms.

Bidding on the silver guitar lasted longest of all. The price rose higher and higher as people bid from all corners of the drawing room.

Finally the auctioneer declared, "Sold to the lady in the pink feathered hat!"

Julie watched in disbelief as Mrs. Buzbee stood up, clapped her hands, and bustled over to stand in front of the guitar while photographers snapped her picture. Over the crowd's applause, Mrs. Buzbee waved to Mr. Vernon and called out, "Feel free to stop by and visit it whenever you like! Come often!"

Mr. Vernon laughed aloud. Julie heard him murmur to his wife, "Something tells me she really means to be friendly rather than nosy."

Mrs. Vernon nodded. "We must make a point of going next door to visit your guitar from time to time."

At the very end of the auction, the chairwoman read out the final tally of funds raised, and the room erupted in applause. "This auction has raised enough to rescue and rehabilitate thousands of seabirds and thousands of acres of oil-coated habitat," she told the cheering audience.

People were standing up to clap now.

With a grin, T. J. slid out of his seat and plugged Mrs. Buzbee's new guitar into its amplifier. The old lady gingerly reached out and plucked a string, and jumped back at the loud twang. "Oh my!" she said, handing the instrument to T. J. Matt let out a whoop as T. J. strummed a dramatic chord on Danny Kendricks's silver guitar.

And Julie, her heart brimming, cheered loudest of all.

LOOKING BACK

A PEEK INTO THE PAST

Auctioned guitar once owned by Jimi Hendrix

Around the time Julie and T. J. were unraveling the mystery of the silver guitar, the music industry was experiencing some big changes. In the 1960s and 1970s, many popular musicians played hard and died young—much like the fictional Danny Kendricks in this book—and their musical instruments and rock memorabilia became very valuable. In 2008, a guitar that had belonged to rock legend Jimi Hendrix sold for over half a million dollars—even though it was nearly ruined from when Hendrix set it on fire at a concert!

Although the money for that guitar did not go to charity, many people have set up auctions and fund-

Jimi Hendrix in concert

raisers to collect money for special causes, much as the Vernons did in the story. In the 1970s, musicians began organizing and playing in benefit concerts to raise awareness and funds for social and environmental causes. In San Francisco, concert promoter Bill Graham organized a concert in Golden Gate Park to raise funds for the city's public-school sports programs, just as the Vernons' first auction did. He called the 1975 concert SNACK—Students Need Athletics, Culture, and Kicks—and invited famous rock bands and musicians like Bob Dylan, the Grateful Dead, and Joan Baez to perform. For kids who played on public-school sports teams, like Julie and T. J., the community's efforts showed them how working together could make a real difference.

Other benefit concerts raised money to help

Folk singer Joni Mitchell performed at Amchitka.

the environment. The 1970 Amchitka concert increased awareness of the environmental damage caused by testing nuclear weapons on the islands of southwestern Alaska. The concert raised $18,000, which funded a boat to sail to the islands and protest the nuclear testing. This protest to protect the marine environment was the first mission of the environmental organization that would later be known as Greenpeace.

In the 1970s, people were beginning to realize how their actions affected the earth and that changes were needed to protect the environment. On April 22, 1970, people celebrated the first Earth Day. On that day, Americans gathered to clean up litter, attend Earth Day fairs, and speak out against pollution. Even elementary schools like Julie's did their part by collecting bottles and paper to recycle and by encouraging students to conserve energy and water.

The next year, the San Francisco Bay Area community stepped into action for the environment once again after two oil tankers collided near the Golden Gate Bridge and spilled a massive amount of oil into the bay. Along with local agencies and adult volunteers, kids like Julie

Bay Area volunteers used hay to absorb some of the oil that washed ashore.

Women clean a pelican with a gentle detergent solution.

and T. J. helped with the cleanup efforts. They put hay bales on the sand to curb the spread of oil and patrolled the beaches to report injured birds and fish. Some collected materials used to clean the oil-drenched shorelines, and others helped clean waterfowl affected by the spill. Thanks to the efforts of the volunteers, agencies, and charitable donors like the Vernons, thousands of birds were cleaned and rehabilitated, and their habitat was gradually restored.

A girl raises money for the National Wildlife Federation to help animals injured by the 2010 oil spill in the Gulf of Mexico.

Today, kids continue to volunteer their time and energy to help make the world better. Girls raise funds for their schools, for animals in need, and for other causes they believe in, just as Julie and her friends did in the 1970s.

Georgia students created these class quilts to raise money at a school auction.

ABOUT THE AUTHOR

Kathryn Reiss was a girl not much older than Julie in the 1970s. She always loved reading mysteries and started writing them herself because nothing mysterious ever seemed to happen in her own neighborhood! Her previous novels of suspense have won many awards. She teaches creative writing at Mills College and lives near San Francisco with her husband and five children.